She made hpeted
hall to her r way.

And utter gasp of horror.

It's blood! she realized. *Blood — smeared all over the wallpaper.*

Brenda felt a surge of dizziness. Her eyes went in and out of focus. When they cleared, she saw to her horror that the dark blood smears spelled out words.

Gripping the doorframe with both hands, she read the words aloud in a trembling whisper:

"SEE YOU ON HALLOWEEN."

Don't miss other Scholastic thrillers
by R.L. Stine:

HALLOWEEN NIGHT

R.L. STINE

SCHOLASTIC INC.
New York Toronto London Auckland Sydney

ISBN 0-590-46098-6

12 11 10 9 8 7 6 5 4 3 2 1   3 4 5 6 7 8/9

Printed in the U.S.A.   01

First Scholastic printing, September, 1993

Chapter 1

Brenda Morgan snapped the rubber band on the Halloween mask, then held it up in front of her face.

Across the room, her friend Traci Warner glanced up from a copy of *Seventeen* and made a disgusted face. "What's that supposed to be? A monster?"

The rubber mask had an enormous eyeball that drooped down to its chin. Green gunk dripped from its nose, and one long tooth poked out between blood-splattered lips.

"No, it's my cousin Halley," Brenda joked.

Dina Smithers, her long legs tucked beneath her on the window seat, had been staring out the window. She turned to inspect Brenda's mask. "Why are you always picking on Halley?"

"I'm not," Brenda replied, poking her fingers

through the eyeholes. "That was a compliment."

Traci laughed and tossed the magazine down on the bed. She brushed her straight black hair behind the shoulders of her green sweater. "Brenda thinks Halley is a monster," she told Dina.

"She *is* a monster," Brenda declared, twirling the mask in her hands.

Dina frowned. She climbed to her feet and stretched, her arms nearly reaching the low ceiling of Brenda's bedroom. Dina was tall and slender, and the black catsuit she wore emphasized her boyish figure. "You should give the poor kid a break," she told Brenda.

"Brenda's just angry because Halley took her room, and she had to move into this closet," Traci said, glancing quickly around the small room.

Brenda let the mask drop to her lap. "It's *not* a closet. I *like* this room," she insisted. "It's . . . cozy."

Tossing her black hair over her shoulders again, Traci raised her eyes to the photographs tacked to the narrow space of wall beside the closet. "You don't even have room for your Luke Perry poster in here," she said.

"I know," Brenda replied unhappily. "I have to go to Halley's room to see it. She wanted to take it down, but I made her keep it."

"It's *her* room now," Dina said, walking over to the dresser mirror and pushing at the sides of her brown hair. "You should let her put up her own posters."

"I like your hair short like that," Traci commented.

"It's too short," Dina complained. "I look like a boy. A really tall boy." Dina was constantly complaining about her looks, about how skinny she was, how her chin was too pointy, her nose too long, how she was taller than most of the boys they knew.

"Why are you always sticking up for Halley?" Brenda demanded, a hint of anger in her voice. "It isn't her room for permanent, you know? Halley's only living here until her stupid parents work out their stupid divorce."

She tossed the monster mask at Dina. It bounced off Dina's shoulder and landed on the white shag rug.

"You're not wearing that mask to your Halloween party, are you?" Traci asked.

A long rectangle of sunlight through the bedroom window made Brenda's copper-colored hair glow. She tugged at the single braid behind her head. "No. It's Randy's mask," she told Traci. Randy was her ten-year-old brother.

"So what's your costume going to be?" Dina asked, still studying herself in the mirror.

"A clown," Brenda replied.

Traci stretched out on Brenda's bed. "You bought a clown costume?"

"No way," Brenda said. "Hey, I'm the costume designer for the senior play, aren't I? I can sew anything. I started sewing it last Saturday. It's going to be the *weirdest* clown costume you ever saw!"

"What's Halley going to be?" Dina asked.

Brenda opened her mouth to answer, but a loud shout interrupted her. "Brenda — turn down that music! I can't hear myself think down here!"

Brenda jumped up at the sound of her mother's voice coming up through the air vent on the floor near the wall. "Sorry, Mom!" she called down.

Dina hurried to the portable stereo on the bookshelf and clicked it off.

"You have to remember to keep it down," Mrs. Morgan called. "The air vent comes down into the hallway. I was sitting in the living room, and I could hear every note!"

"Sorry," Brenda repeated. "I didn't even realize it was on. Really!"

"You girls want anything? Some Cokes or something?" Mrs. Morgan asked.

Brenda peered down. She could see her mother staring up at her through the open air vent. "No thanks, Mom. We're okay."

"Is Halley up there with you?" Mrs. Morgan asked.

"No," Brenda replied, rolling her eyes. "I haven't seen her."

"She promised she'd help me fertilize the rhododendrons this afternoon. I'm so late getting the back yard ready for winter. And your father's been no help at all."

"I haven't seen her," Brenda said curtly.

She waited until she heard her mother's footsteps retreat to the living room. Then she hurried back to her two friends. "Halley's always doing that. She's Little Miss Perfect around my parents. So polite. Always volunteering to help with chores and stuff."

"What's wrong with that?" Dina asked, returning to the window seat. She lowered herself slowly, then crossed her long legs in front of her.

"Halley just does it to make me look bad," Brenda muttered. "When my parents aren't around, she does nothing but complain about them and make fun of them."

"Oh, come on, Brenda. You're not being fair — " Dina accused.

"Oh, yeah?" Brenda insisted. "You should

hear all the jokes Halley makes about how fat my dad is. But when he's around, she's so nice to him, it's disgusting."

"She's probably just nervous," Dina said thoughtfully. "I mean, it would be really hard to have to live away from home, and go to a new school your senior year and everything."

"And Halley's probably really messed up about her parents," Traci added, pulling herself to a sitting position on the bed. "Can you imagine? Your parents going to court and having a battle over who gets to keep you?"

"Like you're property or something," Dina added.

"That could really mess you up," Traci said, shaking her head.

"She's been through a rough time," Brenda admitted, tugging at her copper-colored braid. "But that's no excuse. You two only see her when she's on her best behavior. But she's really mean-natured."

"She has a sarcastic sense of humor, that's all," Dina remarked. "Very dry."

"Very *cold!*" Brenda insisted. "She doesn't have a nice word to say about anyone."

Brenda sighed. Her green eyes seemed to dim. "I don't see why you both are taking her side. She's really awful. I've tried to be nice to her. You know, when she came here last month, I thought it would be kind of neat. Like having a sister my own age. I imagined all the good times Halley and I would have together. But Halley hasn't been friendly at all. It's true!"

Brenda jumped to her feet, pulling down the bottom of her black sweatshirt over her faded jeans. Her friends could see that she was getting worked up. Whenever Brenda got excited, her face turned bright pink, and the freckles on her nose and cheeks darkened.

"Halley and I are the same size," Brenda continued, balling her hands into fists at her sides. "So she's constantly taking my clothes. Without asking. And the other night, she couldn't find her government text. So she took mine and claimed it was hers."

"Hey, calm down, Brenda," Traci said, sliding to the edge of the bed and lowering her feet to the floor.

"I can't calm down!" Brenda cried. "She makes me so mad! I even think she's been flirting with Ted."

Dina scratched her knee through the black tights. "Are you and Ted going to the Homecoming dance?" she asked, obviously trying to change the subject.

"I guess," Brenda answered, her face still pink, her emerald eyes still flashing with anger.

"Noah and I are going to drop by," Traci said, searching for her sneakers under the bed. "But we're probably not going to stay. School dances are always such a bore."

"Do you have a date?" Brenda asked Dina.

Dina lowered her dark eyes. "Huh-uh," she replied quietly.

"Dina's too tall to date," Traci teased.

"Shut up," Dina snapped.

Traci gaped at her, open-mouthed. "Oh, so now you're so sensitive about being tall, we can't even joke about it?"

"It's not a joke," Dina insisted, staring out the window, her lips drawn in a pout. Suddenly, her expression changed. "Hey, look who's coming!"

"Huh? Who?" Brenda rushed to the window, pushing Dina aside so she could see down to the front yard.

"It's Halley," Dina told Traci. "And guess who she's with? Ted."

"I don't believe this," Brenda muttered. "Look how she's grinning at him. Isn't that disgusting? I wish a fly would fly into her mouth!"

Traci laughed. Dina continued to stare out the window as Halley and Ted made their way up the driveway. "It's October," she said softly. "All the flies are dead."

"What are they laughing about?" Brenda asked angrily. "What could be so funny?"

"Calm down, Brenda," Traci said, pulling on her left sneaker. "There's no law against walking with Ted, you know."

"There *should* be a law against that disgusting grin!" Brenda declared. "Maybe her face will crack and disintegrate into a thousand pieces."

Traci snickered. "You're cuter than Halley is," she offered, trying to calm her friend down.

"Cute? I don't *want* to be cute!" Brenda cried. "I'm *sick* of being cute!" She pointed down toward the front yard. "Look at her tossing her blonde hair around! That's so cheap!"

Dina glanced at her watch, and her eyes grew wide with horror. "Oh, no! I'm late for work. Dr. Harper will have a fit!"

"Are you still working in that vet's office?" Traci asked, making a face. "Cleaning up after the poodles?"

Dina didn't reply. She jumped up, pushing nervously at the sides of her short brown hair. "Later, guys."

But before she could reach the doorway, Halley walked in. "Hi, everyone!" She grinned at them, pushing her light blonde hair back off her forehead. She wore tight, straight-legged jeans under a magenta V-necked sweater.

Ted entered the room behind her, glancing at Brenda, then quickly looking away.

"How's it going?" Halley asked. Before anyone could reply, she turned to Brenda. "Can I borrow your car? Just for an hour? Ted offered to give me a driving lesson. Isn't that great? You know how nervous I am about the parking exam."

Brenda's mouth dropped open. Her face turned bright pink, and her freckles darkened. "Borrow the car?"

"You don't mind, do you?" Halley asked, smiling at Ted. "We're just going to drive to the mall parking lot so I can practice parking."

"No. Uh . . . okay," Brenda stammered. Biting her lower lip, she made her way to the dresser and picked up the keys to the little blue Geo her dad had bought her for her seventeenth birthday.

She turned back, her eyes on Ted. He had his hands jammed into his jeans pockets. His mop of curly brown hair was unbrushed, as usual.

Brenda handed the keys to Halley. "Call me later," she told Ted. "After dinner. Maybe we can study the math together."

"Yeah. Good. See you later." He turned and made his way quickly out of the room.

Halley closed her hand around the car keys.

"See you. I'll try not to total it," she said. She hurried after Ted.

Brenda listened to their footsteps going down the stairs. Then she turned to her two friends. "Do you believe it?" she cried. "She takes my boyfriend and my car, and doesn't even say thanks or anything? Do you *believe* it?"

"I have an idea," Traci said, her silvery eyes lighting up with excitement. She stepped up beside Brenda.

"What kind of idea?" Brenda asked skeptically.

"Let's murder her!" Traci suggested.

Chapter 2

"Turn the wheel a little more," Ted instructed. He was twisted in the front passenger seat, craning his neck to peer out the rear window. "Now ease it back slowly."

"Like this?" Halley asked uncertainly. She lowered her foot on the gas pedal, and the back end of the little blue Geo slid partway into the space between two parked cars.

"Whoa!" Ted cried. A second too late. The Geo tapped the bumper of the car parked behind it.

"Oops," Halley said, turning to grin at him. She tossed her blonde hair off her forehead with one hand. Her blue eyes sparkled mischievously.

"Pull it forward a little. Then ease back again," Ted told her. "Here. Put your arm on the back of the seat and turn so you can see better."

He took her hand and raised it to the seat-back. She smiled at him and obediently backed the car out.

They were in a corner of the vast concrete parking lot. There were few cars parked this far away from the stores. The late afternoon sun, glowing red among puffy streaks of white cloud, was lowering itself behind the buildings.

"Am I turning the wheel right?" Halley asked in a tiny voice.

"A little more," Ted instructed. "A little more."

This time she managed to squeeze into the space without bumping anything. "Whew!" Halley sighed loudly and turned to Ted with a pleased smile. "I did it!"

He smiled back at her shyly. She liked the way his eyes crinkled at the corners when he smiled. "Should we try it again?"

"I guess," she replied. "Do you think I'm getting it?"

"Yeah. It isn't so hard," he said, "once you get the back in."

She squeezed the arm of his sweater. "This is really nice of you, Ted. I mean, giving me this lesson."

He blushed and scratched his thick mane of brown hair. "Well, I had an hour free. So . . ." His voice trailed off. He noticed that she hadn't removed her hand from his arm.

"Everyone's been so nice to me," Halley said in a soft voice, her blue eyes studying his face. "I mean, the Morgans have just been great. I don't know what I would have done."

Halley swallowed hard, then continued, her eyes locked on Ted's face. "I couldn't stay at home. Not while my parents were battling it out. It was such a nightmare. Lawyers in and out. My mom and dad shrieking at each other over the phone. Everyone crying all the time."

"That's really . . . bad news," Ted muttered uncomfortably, staring straight ahead at the windshield. He began tapping his right hand nervously against the passenger door.

"Brenda and her friends have been really great, too," Halley continued, squeezing his arm. "I mean, they're not quite what I'm used to. They're . . . uh . . . a little unsophisticated." She giggled. "You won't tell Brenda I said that, will you?"

Ted blushed again. "Said what?" he joked.

"No. They've been great," Halley repeated. "Really."

Across the parking lot, an enormous white truck squealed as it pulled to a stop behind a restaurant. JOHN'S BUNS were the words painted in red and gold on the side panel. Beneath them was a bright painting of a huge hamburger bun.

"That whole truck is filled with buns," Ted said. "Amazing!"

"Wow," Halley said sarcastically. "It doesn't take a whole lot to get you excited, does it!" She laughed.

"Maybe we should practice parallel parking one more time," Ted suggested, glancing at the dashboard clock. "It's getting pretty close to dinnertime."

He tried to pull his arm out from under her hand. As he moved away, his hand brushed her pocketbook, which she had set down between the two seats. The bag toppled over, spilling its contents on the floor at Ted's feet.

"Oh. Sorry." Straining against the seat belt, he leaned forward to pick up her things.

And his eyes settled on a small card inside a clear plastic holder.

He grabbed it and raised it to his face. "Hey — what's this?"

Halley tried to grab it away from him, but Ted had already seen it.

A driver's license with her name — Halley Benson — on it!

"Whoa!" he cried, staring hard at the card. "You already have your license."

"Give me that!" She grabbed it out of his hand. But then her look of distress quickly gave way to an amused smile. Her blue eyes lit up. "It's not a very good picture of me — is it?" she said, studying the small, faded snapshot in the corner of the license.

"I — I don't get it," Ted stammered. "You already have your license. Why did you want a lesson?"

Halley tucked the license into the bag. Then she raised her eyes slowly to Ted's. She wet her lips. Her blonde hair fell over her forehead. "I just wanted to get you alone," she whispered.

Then, before Ted could remove the startled expression from his face, Halley reached over, slid her hands around the back of his neck, and pulled his face down to hers. With a tiny cry, she pressed her warm lips against his, softly at first, then harder.

The kiss lasted a long time.

When it ended, they were both breathing hard. Halley started to remove her hands from Ted's neck. But she changed her mind and pulled him back for another kiss.

"Whoa," he uttered after a long while, pulling his head back. He reached up and gently pulled her hands away. "Whoa."

She giggled mischievously, her eyes gleaming as they stared into his.

"Uh-oh," Ted said. "We shouldn't, you know. I mean . . . we shouldn't."

Then he moved close for another kiss. Her hair fell softly over his face. Somewhere behind them, a car honked. They paid no attention.

When the kiss ended, Halley brushed back her hair and smiled. "Wow," she whispered. "Now what are we going to do about Brenda?"

Chapter 3

"Randy, get lost," Brenda pleaded. "Why are you hanging around here?"

"Because you're so interesting," her brother replied sarcastically. He picked up a little stuffed panda from her dressertop and squeezed it hard.

"Put that down!" Brenda cried. "You're deliberately trying to get me mad."

"It's my hobby," Randy told her, squeezing the bear again until it was almost flat.

Brenda stepped up angrily behind Randy and gripped his shoulders. "Out. Get out," she insisted. "Dina and Traci and I are trying to work."

"No, you're not," Randy replied, allowing Brenda to push him to the door. "You're sitting around, talking about boys as usual."

Traci laughed.

Brenda scowled at her. "Don't encourage him."

"Don't encourage me," Randy repeated. He pulled away from Brenda and made his way to the door, where he turned and tossed the panda. It bounced off Brenda's forehead and fell to the floor.

"Cute," Brenda muttered. "Very cute."

"I know I am," was Randy's closing line. He made a rude noise with his tongue between his lips, and ran down the hall.

Brenda bent to pick up the panda. "Charming, isn't he?" she said sarcastically.

"It runs in the family," Traci joked.

"What's *that* supposed to mean?" Brenda tossed the panda at Traci's head. It missed and bounced off the wall.

"Why does your brother like to hang around us all the time?" Dina asked.

"I think he has a crush on you," Brenda teased.

Dina sighed. "Maybe he could be my date for Homecoming."

"*No way!*" Randy screamed from the hall.

"Get lost, Randy! I mean it!" Brenda shrieked angrily. "Stop listening to every word we say!"

She waited, listening to his footsteps as he

made his way down the stairs. Then she
glanced quickly out her bedroom window.

It was a gray afternoon. The first cold day
of fall, so cold that her father had turned the
furnace on for the first time.

Traci and Dina had come over after lunch to
work on their writing project. But so far they
hadn't gotten any work done because Randy
was being such a pest.

Dina, dressed in maroon sweats, had taken
her usual place on the window seat, her long
legs tucked beneath her. Traci, in black tights
and an oversized white sweater, stretched out
on the white shag rug. Brenda, after returning
the battered panda to its place on the dresser,
sat down on the edge of the bed. She was wearing faded jeans and an orange T-shirt under a
green T-shirt.

"Did you go out with Ted last night?" Dina
asked her.

Brenda nodded. She picked up the costume
she'd been working on when her friends had
arrived and began stitching a sleeve.

"You go somewhere or just hang around?"
Traci asked.

"We didn't do much," Brenda said, frowning.
"Ted seemed really . . . distracted. I mean, he
barely said a word. Like his mind was on something else." She shrugged and kept sewing.

"Weird," Traci muttered.

"He can be like that sometimes," Dina said matter-of-factly.

Brenda gazed up at her friend. She had forgotten that Dina had gone out with Ted for a while when they were juniors.

"Noah and I went to that Clint Eastwood movie," Traci offered. "It was so violent, I couldn't believe it. Noah loved it."

"Sounds like Noah," Dina said dryly. "And what's new with Halley?" she asked Brenda, staring out the window. "You two getting along any better?"

"I guess," Brenda replied, concentrating on her stitches. "We really haven't talked much. I kind of get the feeling she's been avoiding me. Which is fine with me." She adjusted the sleeve, then resumed sewing. "Every time we *do* run into each other, Halley has had the strangest smile on her face."

"What kind of smile?" Traci asked, sitting up straight on the rug, pulling her black hair behind her head in a ponytail, then letting it go.

"I can't really describe it," Brenda said. "It's like she has a secret or something. You know. A really smug smile."

"So are we really going to murder her?" Traci asked.

"Yeah. Let's!" Brenda replied, chuckling. "I'll really enjoy that."

"That's really sick," Dina objected, lowering her feet to the floor and leaning forward on the window seat. "I mean, what happens when she finds out?"

"We'll tell her it was just a joke," Brenda said.

"But she'll really be hurt," Dina insisted.

"I know. Let's murder Ted, too," Brenda said with growing excitement.

"Great! A double murder!" Traci exclaimed, clapping her hands.

Dina gazed at Brenda, a shocked expression on her face. "You really want to murder Ted?"

"Why not?" Brenda asked casually.

"Mrs. Ryland is a cool teacher," Traci said. "She really thinks of great assignments."

"If only she could find pants that fit," Brenda said, snickering. "What's with those baggy bottoms?"

They all laughed. "It's just the way she's built, I think," Dina offered. "But she's a cool teacher. Especially for an English teacher. I mean, this is a great writing assignment."

"Well, plotting a murder mystery isn't going to be that easy," Brenda replied thoughtfully. "I mean, we know who we want for our victims.

But now we need suspects. And clues. And a detective or something."

"I think *we* should be the detectives in the story," Dina suggested, climbing to her feet and bending from side to side in an impromptu aerobics limbering exercise.

"No way!" Traci protested. "We have to be the murderers!"

"Three murderers?" Brenda asked. "Three murderers for two murders?"

"Well . . ." Traci frowned, thinking hard. "Yeah," she said finally. "Thinking up a good murder plot is going to be harder than I thought. I mean, we can't just have someone shoot Halley and Ted. We have to think up something more clever."

"Strangling," Brenda suggested quietly. "Strangling would be good. For Halley, anyway."

"Not clever enough," Traci said, playing with her hair.

"Yeah. We need plot twists," Dina agreed, still exercising. "You know. Some surprises." She stopped for a moment. "What did Mrs. Ryland call them? Red herrings?"

"Yeah. Things to fool the reader, throw them off the track," Brenda said. "Like false clues. And false suspects. Hey — I know!" She held up the clown costume she was sewing.

"The murderer is a clown?" Traci asked, confused.

"No. Let's make it a Halloween murder," Brenda suggested. "You know. At a costume party."

"Ooh — that's great!" Traci declared.

"You mean, everyone's in costume, right?" Dina asked, dropping back onto the window seat. "And so there's no way to know who the murderer is?"

"Yeah," Brenda said enthusiastically. "And Halley is in costume, too. And she gets stabbed or something."

"Maybe Ted stabs Halley," Traci suggested.

"Maybe," Brenda said, tilting her head, a habit she had whenever she was thinking hard about something. "And since everyone is in costume, and it's a really crowded party — "

"Like yours is going to be," Traci interrupted.

"I don't like this," Dina broke in. "I mean, it's too real or something."

"Huh? What do you mean?" Brenda asked, lowering the clown costume to her lap and reaching for the unfinished sleeve.

"I mean it's too real. It's kind of giving me the creeps," Dina told her with a shudder. She pushed nervously at her short, brown hair.

"Maybe we shouldn't use real names. Maybe we should just make up people. It's supposed to be fiction, right?"

"Yeah. That's true," Traci agreed.

"But it'll be so much more satisfying to kill Halley off!" Brenda argued. "Even if it's only on paper."

"But it's so mean!" Dina cried. "Someone will tell her. She's bound to find out, Brenda."

Brenda shrugged. "You think it's mean because you don't have to live with her. *She's* the one who's mean. Ask Randy. Even Randy thinks she's mean."

Brenda stared suspiciously at Dina. "Hey — why are you always sticking up for Halley?"

"Huh?" Dina reacted with surprise. "I'm not. Really. I just think . . . well, I just think that you're not being very understanding. Halley is obviously going through a really terrible time. I'll bet she's totally messed up about her parents. I remember when *my* parents split up, and . . ." Her voice trailed off.

Suddenly, a flood of memories swept over Brenda. *I completely forgot,* she realized. *Dina went through the same thing. Dina's parents had a terrible custody battle over her. And Dina freaked out or something.*

How could I have forgotten all that? Brenda asked herself, staring hard at Dina.

No wonder Dina always takes Halley's side. Dina has been through the same nightmare.

"You two probably don't remember what I went through," Dina said with surprising bitterness. She turned away from Brenda and Traci and stared out the window. Then, suddenly, her mouth dropped open, and she uttered a low gasp.

"Dina, what *is* it?" Brenda asked, jumping to her feet.

Dina didn't reply. She stared down to the driveway, her mouth still hanging open.

"Dina? What's out there?" Brenda demanded.

"Uh . . . nothing," Dina started to say.

But Brenda and Traci both rushed up beside her. Their knees on the window seat, they pressed their faces to the window and stared down.

There in the driveway stood Ted's old Honda Civic.

It took Brenda a while to focus on what she was seeing. It all appeared to be happening in slow motion.

At first, she saw the gray glare of clouds reflected on the windshield. Then the back of Halley's head came into view.

All that blonde hair, Brenda thought.

What is Halley doing?

She's sitting in the passenger seat, but she's leaning over to the driver's side.

Brenda stared for the longest time at the back of Halley's head. And, finally, the whole picture came into focus behind the glare on the windshield.

And she realized with a jolt that ran down her entire body that Halley was kissing Ted.

Uttering a loud gasp, Brenda pulled back from the window and jumped to her feet. "I'll murder Halley for real!" she cried. "I really will!"

Chapter 4

The next morning Brenda awoke early to the rumble and clatter of a garbage truck somewhere down the block. She sat up and squinted toward the window. The patch of sky she could see was charcoal-gray. Dark clouds hovered menacingly.

She had an impulse to settle back down, pull the covers over her head, and hide in bed all day. But she knew her mother would be calling up the stairs any second. There was no way Brenda could hide.

She pulled on a pair of black tights, struggling with them, still half-asleep. Then she found a short black skirt to go over them. A long-sleeved black crew-neck top completed the outfit.

I might as well wear black, she thought bitterly. It suits my mood perfectly.

She hurried downstairs to the kitchen where

her mother was pouring water into the coffee-maker. "Mom, I really have to talk to you," Brenda whispered urgently, after making sure Halley wasn't lurking about.

"Well, good morning to you, too!" her mother exclaimed sarcastically. Mrs. Morgan was a plump, pleasant-looking woman with jagged streaks of white in her short, black hair, and dramatic dark eyes that, to Brenda, always seemed to see right through people. She was already dressed in loose-fitting jeans and a pale blue denim shirt.

"Good morning, Mom," Brenda said impatiently. "I have to talk to you about Halley."

Brenda's mother sighed and crossed her arms in front of her chest. "Not again, Bren."

"No. Really, Mom," Brenda insisted shrilly. "She's — she's ruining my life!"

Mrs. Morgan frowned. "Brenda, we've had this discussion before, remember? I told you to be patient with Halley. It's *her* life that's being ruined, you know."

"Mom — "

Her mother raised a hand. "No. Stop. You and Halley are seniors in high school. You should be able to solve your own differences and get along. You shouldn't have to come running to me like a ten-year-old — "

"But — but — " Brenda sputtered. And

then she blurted out, "Why do you always take *her* side?"

She knew she sounded babyish. She couldn't help it.

Halley had taken her room, her clothes . . . and now her boyfriend. And Halley was supposed to be given all the understanding, all the sympathy — just because her parents were going through a messy divorce and staging a big custody battle for her.

I'll bet her parents are fighting *not* to keep her, Brenda thought bitterly. Her mother wants her father to have custody of Halley, and her father wants her mother to have custody.

Brenda snickered at the thought.

"What are you laughing about?" her mother asked suspiciously.

"Nothing," Brenda replied curtly. "So you're not going to listen to me?"

Mrs. Morgan shook her head. "Settle it with Halley. Don't make me choose sides."

"But I'm your *daughter*!" Brenda screamed.

At that moment, Halley entered, a bright smile on her freshly scrubbed face. "Morning everyone!" she chirped.

Brenda uttered a loud, exasperated groan and stormed out of the kitchen.

* * *

The halls of McKinley High rang with shouts and laughter at the end of school that afternoon. Lockers slammed. Two boys were tossing a Notre Dame cap back and forth, and a third boy, most likely the cap's owner, was trying to snatch it from them.

Brenda stepped out of her seventh-period study hall and bumped right into Dina, who was struggling to get her bulging backpack zipped. "Hi!" Brenda cried in surprise.

"Bad day," Dina muttered, frowning. "I read the wrong pages for the Spanish exam."

"Wow, that's bad news," Brenda sympathized, shaking her head.

"Then I spilled half a sloppy joe on my shirt at lunch," Dina cried, pointing to the dark brown stain that streaked down her pale yellow blouse.

"At least the colors match," Brenda said dryly. She chuckled.

"I'm not going to laugh at that," Dina told her sharply. "You always think it's a riot when something bad happens to me."

"Not *always*," Brenda teased. "Listen, can you come to my house now to work on the murder plot? We've really got to do some hard thinking about it."

"I can't," Dina answered unhappily, hoisting

the heavy backpack onto her slender shoulders. "I have to go to my job on Mondays."

"We're never going to figure this murder out," Brenda moaned. "It's due right after Halloween."

"I could come over after work," Dina suggested. "About eight?"

"Okay, good," Brenda said. "I'll call Traci and tell her to come, too. See you."

Dina headed away, hunched under the weight of her backpack. Brenda went jogging back to her. "By the way, what's your costume going to be? You know. For my party."

Dina sighed. "I don't know. I think I'm just going to be a monk."

"Huh? A *what*?" Brenda demanded.

"A monk," Dina repeated. "I found this huge old brown bathrobe with a hood in my mom's closet. I guess it used to belong to my dad. It looks like a perfect monk's robe." She dodged two cheerleaders who came running at full speed toward the gym. "I'm not good at sewing and stuff like you and Traci," she added, almost apologetically.

"Sounds like a comfortable costume," Brenda told her. "I'm going to sweat like a pig in mine."

Dina said something in reply, but it was lost among the shouts and laughter in the crowded hallway. Brenda watched Dina disappear out the double front doors. Then she turned the corner to head to her locker.

And stopped.

There was Halley near the end of the hall. Brenda recognized the blonde hair first, so messy, falling down over Halley's eyes.

Halley was leaning against a closed locker. She had her hands on a boy's shoulders. She was smiling at him with red-lipsticked lips.

And the boy was Noah. Traci's boyfriend.

Brenda froze in the middle of the corridor and stared.

Noah and Halley were laughing about something. She pretended to slap his face. Just let her hand glide over his cheek. Didn't really hit him.

Noah's normally pale skin turned bright pink. He was about three inches shorter than Halley. He had straw-colored hair, cut very short with yellow sideburns. He was wearing a silver and blue McKinley High jacket, with a big silver M on the front, the letter he had won on the wrestling team.

He gave Halley a playful shove. She shoved him back. They laughed. Halley started to walk away.

I don't believe this, Brenda thought.

First she's kissing Ted right in *my* driveway.

And now she's coming on to Traci's boyfriend in front of the whole school.

What is her *problem*?

I have to find Traci, Brenda thought, her mind racing feverishly. I have to tell her.

No! She argued with herself. I *can't* tell her.

Two teachers hurried past, talking about last Friday's McKinley football game. "Did you see the size of Wakely's fullback?" one of them said. "Do they give him steroids, or do they just inflate him?"

The halls were growing quieter as students headed out the door. A girl called to Brenda, and she turned to say hi.

When she turned back, Brenda saw that Noah was alone now. And he was staring down the hall at her.

As he started toward her, moving quickly with his lumbering gait, she had an impulse to run. But he was in front of her before she could get her legs moving.

"Brenda — hi!" he said, with false enthusiasm. His round cheeks were dotted with large, bright red circles. His forehead was perspiring. His tiny dark eyes studied her face. He had his hands jammed into the pockets of his letter jacket.

"Hi, Noah," Brenda replied coldly.

"I . . . uh . . . saw you watching us," Noah said, a nervous grin spreading across his round face. He wiped his short blond hair back with a pudgy hand.

"Yeah," Brenda replied, shifting her backpack on her shoulders.

"Listen, Brenda — " Noah started, his grin fading. He leaned toward her, as if making sure she knew he was being confidential. "Halley and I — we were just talking, you know? I mean, that's all. We're in the same math class. We came out, and we were just kidding around. About math."

"Uh-huh," Brenda replied flatly.

"So you don't have to run and tell Traci that I was coming on to Halley or anything. Okay?" Noah's expression had turned pleading. Brenda had the feeling he might drop to his knees and *beg* her not to tell Traci.

She stared at his sweating face for a long moment. *What on earth does Traci see in him?* she wondered.

What does Halley see?

"Hey, I won't say anything," she assured Noah. "I'm not a cop or something."

Noah laughed, a bit too loudly and too long. He had a high-pitched laugh that set Brenda's teeth on edge. "You don't *look* like a cop!" he exclaimed.

"Is that supposed to be a compliment?" Brenda shot back.

Noah grew serious again. "It's just that I know you and Traci are best friends, and . . . well . . ."

"I'm not going to run to Traci every time you talk to a girl in the hall," Brenda told him. "Listen, I've got to get home."

"Yeah. Okay." He looked very relieved. "See you." He started down the hall, then stopped. "Hey, your cousin's really nice. You know?"

Brenda didn't answer. She gave Noah a wave, turned, and headed to her locker.

Halley must be boy-crazy, Brenda thought.

First Ted. Then Noah. And tonight she had a study date at another boy's house.

Is she trying to win over every boy in school?

Seated at her small oak desk, Brenda stared down at her history text. The tensor lamp threw down a cone of white light onto the page that seemed to make the words shrivel and blur.

I can't concentrate on this stuff, Brenda thought unhappily. I can't concentrate on anything tonight.

I have to force Halley from my mind. I *have* to stop thinking about her.

Traci had come over right after dinner, eager

to get started on the murder mystery plot. Brenda was dying to tell her about seeing Noah and Halley in the hall together, how they laughed together, how Halley put her hands all over Noah's face and shoulders as if she owned him.

Somehow Brenda held it in. But it drove her crazy the entire evening, made her feel tense and uncomfortable. It must have shown because at one point Traci asked, "What's wrong with you tonight?" And Brenda made up some dumb excuse about being nervous about an exam.

Dina had arrived a little after eight. The three girls had sat around Brenda's room, trying to plot their Halloween murder. With little success.

"I'm just not inspired tonight," Traci admitted.

"Me, either," Dina quickly agreed. She yawned. "I'm too tired to murder anyone tonight."

"Let's try again tomorow," Brenda suggested. "Think about it, okay? We'll all come with ideas tomorrow. I'm sure we can think of a good way to murder Halley. We *have* to."

A few minutes after Traci and Dina had left, Ted called. "Brenda, I have to talk to you."

Those were the only words she let him get

out. As soon as she recognized his voice, Brenda slammed the receiver down.

Her heart pounding, her mind churning with angry thoughts, she had stared at the phone on her desk and pictured Ted's car parked in her driveway, and the messy blonde hair, Halley's blonde hair, over Ted's face as they kissed. Kissed right under Brenda's bedroom window.

No way I'm talking to you, Ted, Brenda thought bitterly.

No way!

She lowered her head, leaned over the desk, and stared down at the blur of tiny words on the page of the textbook.

I can't read this, she thought. My eyes just keep watering over. Maybe I should set my alarm, get up early, and read it in the morning when I'm fresh.

Yes.

She slammed the book shut. The book had been carefully wrapped in a brown paper cover on the first day of school. Brenda had penciled a heart on the front. Inside were two names: Brenda and Ted.

Shaking her head, she lifted a pencil from the cup in the corner of her desk and crossed out Ted's name. Then she clicked off the tensor lamp and started to get up.

She glanced at the clock on her dresser: nearly eleven.

Then her eyes went to the bedroom window across the room.

And Brenda saw the man's face staring in at her, his eyes bulging, his mouth wide in an ugly, leering grin.

And she opened her mouth to scream.

Chapter 5

The man's bulging eyes stared at Brenda through the glass without blinking.

As Brenda screamed, he didn't react. His face remained set in its ghastly open-mouthed expression, as if he were mimicking her horror.

She heard footsteps on the stairs.

"Brenda — what's the matter?" Her mother's voice called shrilly.

Brenda's scream ended in a choked cough.

The man still hadn't moved.

As she stared at the bulging eyes, she realized he couldn't move. He wasn't real.

She lurched to the window and pulled it open.

The face was a cardboard cutout. Some sort of mask. Taped to the outside of the window.

With a trembling hand, Brenda pulled the face off the window.

"Brenda — what happened?" Mrs. Morgan burst into the room, followed by Randy and Halley. "I heard a scream and — "

Brenda held up the ugly cardboard face. "I — I'm sorry," she stammered. "This face. It was in the window, and, well . . . I thought it was a man."

Randy laughed. Halley tossed her hair behind her head, her eyebrows knit in bewilderment, a frown on her lipsticked lips.

"You thought a man was up here?" Mrs. Morgan asked. "On the second floor?"

"He stared at me," Brenda exclaimed, still holding the cutout face in front of her. "I looked up and — " Her eyes fell to the back of the mask. Something was written there. "Hey — "

"Brenda, you scared me to death!" her mother said with a sigh, shaking her head, raising her hand to her heart.

"Me, too!" Randy cried, giggling.

"Someone wrote something on the back," Brenda told them. "It says, 'See You on Halloween.' "

Brenda tossed the mask onto her dressertop and glared at Randy. "Funny joke," she muttered angrily.

Randy stopped giggling. "Hey — don't look at *me*, Bren!" He backed up toward the bedroom door. "I didn't do it!"

Brenda took a few steps toward him, her expression menacing. "Come on, Randy. Confess."

"Randy, did you deliberately scare your sister like that?" Mrs. Morgan demanded.

"No way!" Randy protested. But a broad smile spread over his face. "I didn't put that mask there. Really!"

"Then why are you grinning?" Brenda asked.

"I'm just grinning, that's all. But I didn't do it, Brenda. I *didn't*!" Randy cried.

Brenda turned her gaze on Halley. Halley had an amused expression on her face as she watched Brenda accuse Randy.

"Hey, don't look at me," Halley said, catching Brenda's accusing stare. "Why would I tape a dumb mask to your window?"

"It was just a silly joke," Mrs. Morgan said. "Why are you so upset, Brenda?"

"I — I — " Brenda was beginning to feel a little foolish. "I guess I'm a little jumpy or something," she muttered, still glaring at Halley.

Halley did it, Brenda thought. *Just to make me look like a fool.*

I can tell by the pleased expression on her face.

Halley did it.

"Really! What a fuss over nothing," Mrs. Morgan declared. She turned and followed Randy out the door.

As usual, she's on Halley's side, Brenda thought bitterly.

Halley quickly said good-night to Brenda and hurried out the door. "I hope you don't have bad dreams because of it," she said, a smug smile on her face.

Brenda didn't reply. When everyone had left, she picked up the mask and examined the back again.

" 'See You on Halloween.' " She read the scrawled words again and again.

What did it mean? she wondered.

Was it just Randy or Halley playing a dumb joke?

Or was something really strange going on?

Brenda plunged her hands deep into the wet, orange goo. "Yum!" she declared happily. She pulled out a handful and tossed it onto the newspaper spread out over the kitchen table.

"Yuck!" Traci declared. "It's really gross."

"Yeah!" Randy cried excitedly. "Can I try it? Can I help?"

"I guess," Brenda replied reluctantly. "Just don't start throwing it or acting stupid, okay?"

Randy scooted behind the kitchen table and pushed his way between Brenda and Traci. He eagerly plunged one hand into the opening on top of the pumpkin, and a devilish grin spread over his face.

"Randy — I warned you!" Brenda cried.

"Okay, okay." He pulled out a handful of pumpkin. "I hate the smell!" he declared, making a face.

"Save the seeds," Traci said. "We can roast them when we're finished."

"I'll get a big spoon," Brenda said, pushing away from the table. "We've got to really scrape this pumpkin clean, or else it'll start to smell."

Randy pulled out another handful of pumpkin seeds. Then he picked up one of the big kitchen knives and raised it above his head as if preparing to attack Traci.

"Randy — put that down!" Brenda scolded, returning with a large metal spoon. "Those knives are for carving."

"I can carve," Randy insisted. "I'm good at carving."

"Traci and I are going to do the carving," Brenda told him firmly. She took the big knife from his sticky, pumpkiny hand.

"Hi, everyone." Dina appeared in the kitchen doorway, wearing a heavy white sweater over black jeans. "Sorry I'm late. Emergency at the animal clinic and I had to stay late."

"You look tired," Traci told Dina as she joined them at the kitchen table. "You've got circles under your eyes."

"I *am* tired," Dina confessed with a sigh. "I wish I could quit this job, but we really need the money. My dad lost his job, and he hasn't been able to send Mom and me a penny."

"I'll give you a penny," Randy offered, grinning.

"Is that your idea of a joke?" Brenda snapped.

"Yeah," he replied.

"I can't believe you're carving a jack-o'-lantern already," Dina said, pulling off the heavy sweater to reveal a maroon turtleneck underneath. "Your party isn't for two more weeks. It'll rot!"

"This is a practice jack-o'-lantern," Brenda told her. "I want to have a lot of jack-o'-lanterns at the party. You know. All with candles in them."

"That'll look great," Dina said.

"Can we let it rot?" Randy asked.

"Brenda's so nervous about this party," Traci told Dina. "That's why we're doing a practice jack-o'-lantern."

"I'm . . . I'm nervous about everything lately," Brenda said wistfully, tilting the pumpkin to scrape at the inside with the metal spoon.

The mask of the man with bulging eyes flashed into her mind. She had an impulse to tell Traci and Dina about it. But she decided they'd just laugh at her.

"I'm nervous about our murder mystery," Dina said. "We don't have a single idea yet."

"Maybe we can use a jack-o'-lantern in it," Traci suggested. "You know. The murderer slips a jack-o'-lantern over his face — "

" — and grins the victim to death!" Brenda interrupted.

"That's dumb," Randy said.

"There. I think it's all cleaned out," Brenda said, putting down the spoon. She wiped a gob of pumpkin off her cheek with the back of her hand. "Now, I want to draw the face on before we start to carve."

"What's it going to look like? Like *you*?" Randy asked his sister.

Brenda started to reply. But she stopped with her mouth open as an enormous figure filled the doorway, blocking out the light from the hall.

It's a gorilla! Brenda realized, feeling a shock of surprise tighten her throat.

Before she could cry out, the enormous animal lumbered to the table and grabbed a kitchen knife in its hairy hand, raising it menacingly over the pumpkin.

Chapter 6

"Ohh!" Brenda uttered a startled cry and grabbed at the knife.

But the creature swung its arm away, holding tightly to the knife.

Traci and Dina both cried out. Randy ducked under the table.

The gorilla lowered the knife. Then it raised a hand to the crown of its head, tugged hard, and pulled off its head.

Halley's grinning face was revealed. She shook her head to free her mane of blonde hair, which had been tucked tightly into the costume.

"Like it?" she asked.

Brenda was still breathing hard. She waited for her heart to stop pounding. "Where — where'd you get that gorilla costume?" she finally managed to ask her cousin.

Halley's blue eyes sparkled excitedly. She

had scared Brenda, and she knew it and seemed to enjoy it. "Upstairs. In the attic. Uncle Michael showed it to me. It was in an old trunk."

"I knew it was just a costume," Randy said, bobbing up from under the table.

"It's a *great* costume!" Traci declared. "It's so hairy."

"Yeah," Dina agreed. "It looks so real."

"I'm going to wear it to your party," Halley said, turning around in a circle to model it. "It's perfect." She set the head down on the kitchen counter. "I didn't scare you — did I, Brenda?"

"No. I was just . . . surprised," Brenda replied. "It's a great costume," she admitted. "I've never seen it before. I wonder why Dad never showed it to *me*."

Halley scratched her armpits like a monkey and, hopping up and down, uttered some gorilla grunts, grinning at Randy. Then she glanced at the kitchen clock above the stove and her expression changed. "Can I borrow your car, Bren?"

"Huh?" The question caught Brenda by surprise. She had loaned her precious blue Geo to Halley and Ted once. But she didn't want Halley to make a habit of driving it. After all, it was Brenda's.

"I'll be really careful," Halley said, putting her hairy gorilla hands together in a begging pose. "I promised I'd meet someone at the mall, and your parents took their car. Please, Bren?"

Brenda saw that both Traci and Dina were eyeing her, waiting to see how she'd react. And she decided she really had no choice.

"Sure, Halley," she replied. "Take the car. The keys are on the table in the front entry-way."

"Thanks," Halley said. Tucking the gorilla mask under her arm, she padded out of the kitchen. Brenda could hear her heavy footsteps on the stairs as she hurried up to her room to change.

"That was nice of you," Traci told Brenda, a note of surprise in her voice.

"*Too* nice," Dina added in a low voice.

"Oh!" Brenda cried out as she felt a sharp pain shoot through her hand. She lowered her eyes and saw a trickle of bright red blood on the newspaper beside the pumpkin.

It took her a while to realize that she had been gripping one of the kitchen knives by the blade and had cut her finger. "Now why did I do that?" she cried, more to herself than the others. She wrapped the finger in a paper towel and hurried to the bathroom to get a bandage for it.

When she returned to the kitchen, Traci and Dina were busy with black markers drawing a

face onto the front of the hollowed-out pumpkin. Randy had deserted them and gone to the
den to watch television.

"Do you like this face?" Traci asked, tilting
the pumpkin so Brenda could see it better.

"Pretty good," Brenda replied. She pulled a
pumpkin seed from Traci's straight black hair.
"Make the teeth bigger. They'll be easier to
carve."

"Halley really scared me, bursting in like
that in that ugly costume," Dina admitted.

"I think she *wanted* to scare us," Traci replied, drawing bigger teeth on the pumpkin.

"Lots of scares around here lately," Brenda
said wistfully. "You should've been here *last*
night!" She told them about the mask taped to
the outside of her bedroom window with the
message scrawled on the other side.

"That was one of Randy's little jokes, right?"
Dina asked.

Brenda shook her head. "I don't think so.
Randy swears he didn't do it." She stopped
talking as she heard Halley's footsteps in the
front hallway. She heard the jingle of car keys,
then the front door slammed behind Halley.

"I think Halley did it," Brenda said, whis-
pering even though her cousin had left the
house.

"Huh? Why?" Traci demanded, finishing the

new teeth and reaching for a carving knife. "Why would Halley do a dumb thing like that?"

Brenda shrugged. "Beats me. Why does Halley do anything?"

"Give the poor kid a break," Dina muttered.

"Let's change the subject," Brenda said sharply. "I've been thinking about our murder plot."

Traci dug the knife blade into the pumpkin and began carefully slicing out the first triangular eye. "You have an idea about how Halley is going to get it?"

"Well," Brenda said, picking up two pumpkin seeds and rolling them around in her hand, "I still like the idea of making it a Halloween murder."

"Yeah. That's cool," Traci replied with immediate enthusiasm.

"It should take place at a costume party, just like the one you're going to have," Dina said, pushing at the sides of her short, brown hair.

"That's what *I'm* thinking," Brenda said. "Everyone is in costume, see. And Halley is in her gorilla costume."

"And someone feeds her a poison banana!" Traci exclaimed.

Brenda and Dina laughed.

"We need something bloodier," Brenda said. Traci pulled the knife from the pumpkin, raised it high, and made some quick, stabbing motions with it. "Chop, chop," she said, smiling.

"Yeah. That's better," Brenda cried. "I like the idea that she's stabbed right through the big, hairy gorilla suit."

"And no one knows she's been stabbed," Dina offered.

"Huh?" Brenda reacted with surprise. She tossed the two pumpkin seeds onto the pile on the newspaper. "I don't get it."

"The costume is so thick and heavy, no one knows she's been stabbed," Dina explained. "She's sitting in a chair. And everyone thinks she's just sitting there enjoying the party — until they see this blood stain start to grow bigger and bigger, and — "

"No. How about this? The costume starts to fill up with blood," Traci suggested excitedly. "I mean, like, all of Halley's blood pours out into the costume, and it's like a big water balloon, only it's filled with blood."

"Yuck!" Brenda cried, making a disgusted face. "Gross!"

"I like it!" Dina declared quietly.

"We need some kind of trick," Brenda said, squeezing the bandage on her cut finger. "Something really clever. You know. You think you know who killed Halley, but it turns out to be someone completely different."

"How about Ted?" Traci asked, cutting into the triangular nose of the pumpkin. "How about if Ted is the murderer?"

"Leave him out of it," Brenda said sharply. "He's not invited."

"Have you talked to Ted?" Dina asked.

"No way," Brenda insisted, shaking her head. "No way I'll *ever* talk to him again. The creep." She could feel her face growing red.

"Did you tell Halley you saw her and Ted?" Traci asked.

Brenda's face grew even hotter. "I try to talk to Halley as little as possible."

"So Ted's not invited to your party?" Dina asked.

"Huh-uh," Brenda said, picking up the pumpkin seeds again. "No way."

"So then we *definitely* should murder him in our story!" Traci said, concentrating on her carving.

"He called me, but I hung up on him," Brenda told them. "Then he tried to talk to me in the lunchroom this afternoon. But I ran out the door. I think maybe he got the hint." She uttered a quiet sob. "I can't believe Halley would do that to me."

Traci was halfway finished with the mouth. "Anyone else want to carve?"

"Finish it," Dina told her. "You're doing a neat job." She turned to Brenda. "I hope Halley didn't just borrow your car to go meet Ted."

The idea hadn't occurred to Brenda. She clenched her teeth so hard, her jaw hurt. "I hope not," she said darkly. "For both of their sakes."

Brenda glanced down at her injured finger. "Oh, no." Dark blood was seeping through the bandage. "I hope I don't need stitches on this thing. I'm going upstairs and put on a new bandage."

"I'm almost finished with the mouth," Traci called after her.

"Great. When I come back, we can clean up," Brenda said. She hurried up the stairs, holding her finger, thinking about Halley and Ted.

She wouldn't borrow my car to go meet my boyfriend — would she?

Upstairs, Brenda saw that the lights were on in her bedroom.

That's strange, she thought. She didn't remember leaving them on.

She made her way down the narrow, carpeted hall to her room and stopped in the doorway.

And uttered a loud gasp of horror.

It's blood! she realized. *Blood — smeared all over the wallpaper.*

Brenda felt a surge of dizziness. Her eyes went in and out of focus. When they cleared, she saw to her horror that the dark blood smears spelled out words.

Gripping the doorframe with both hands, she read the words aloud in a trembling whisper: " 'SEE YOU ON HALLOWEEN.' "

Chapter 7

"Halley did it. I know she did," Brenda said in a trembling voice. She drummed her fingers nervously on the tabletop.

"So what happened when your parents got home?" Traci asked. "Did they freak?"

Brenda nodded, brushing a strand of copper-colored hair off her forehead. "My dad wanted to call the police."

It was a blustery night. The two girls were seated across from one another in a red vinyl booth near the rear of Mulligan's, an enormous ice-cream restaurant at the mall.

The restaurant was crowded despite the threatening weather outside. Brenda seldom went out on a school night. But tonight she'd decided she just *had* to get out of the house. Traci had picked her up a little after seven-thirty. They had cruised aimlessly around town for a while, and ended up at Mulligan's.

Traci sipped her chocolate ice-cream soda through a straw, her eyes on Brenda's troubled face. Brenda ignored the dish of Heath Bar Crunch she had ordered. She fiddled with the spoon or drummed her fingers on the table, and kept glancing quickly around the large room, hoping not to see anyone she knew.

"So did you tell them it was Halley?" Traci demanded, spooning up a chunk of chocolate ice cream from the tall soda glass.

"Yes." Brenda replied. "But of course they didn't believe me." She sighed unhappily. "They don't want to believe me. They always take Halley's side. Always!" She stabbed the mound of ice cream with her spoon.

"What happened when — " Traci started.

But Brenda interrupted her. "My dad said, 'Where would Halley get all that blood?' "

Traci dropped her spoon. "You mean it was *real blood* on your wall? It wasn't red paint?"

Brenda shook her head. Her eyes revealed anger mixed with fear. "It was real blood, Traci. She smeared real blood on my wall. Isn't that sick?"

Traci swallowed hard. "What is she — some sort of vampire or something?"

Brenda didn't reply. She lowered her eyes

to the table. She appeared lost in her thoughts.

"Could it have been your little brother?" Traci asked.

"No," Brenda answered quickly. She raised her eyes to Traci's. "Where would Randy get blood? Besides, he isn't tall enough. The words started nearly up at the ceiling." She picked up the spoon and let it drop back onto the ice cream. "Randy is a goof, but he wouldn't do anything vicious like that."

A loud crash made both girls jump. One of the waitresses had dropped a tray of dirty dishes.

Music boomed from the jukebox inside the front entrance. Someone had played an old Guns 'n Roses song. Six teenage boys had squeezed into a booth near the front and were playing air guitar and singing along.

Traci leaned forward over the table so that Brenda could hear her over the noise. "So what happened when Halley got home last night?"

"Nothing," Brenda replied glumly. "She acted horrified. She got all pale and acted as if she couldn't believe it."

"And your parents believed her? Didn't they question her or accuse her or *anything*?"

Brenda shook her head. "No. Nothing." She dropped the spoon onto the tabletop. "I know she did it, Traci. We all heard her go upstairs last night. I know that's when she did it. While we were working on the pumpkin. But my mom and dad" — her voice broke — "They don't want to hear a word against Halley."

Traci nibbled at her lower lip, her expression thoughtful. "But why would Halley do it?" she asked finally.

Brenda shook her head and shrugged. "Because she's sick, I guess. This whole divorce thing has just messed her up." She paused for a long moment. "Maybe she's jealous of me. You know. Because I have a normal family." She frowned. "I don't know, Traci. I really don't. It's crazy. Just crazy."

"Did you talk to Dina tonight?" Traci asked, spooning up another mound of ice cream from her glass.

"She's working late," Brenda told her. "Poor Dina. She looks so tired, doesn't she? I think she should quit this job, don't you? It's too many hours, and — "

Brenda suddenly realized that Traci wasn't listening to her. Traci was staring over Brenda's shoulder, her face frozen in wide-eyed shock.

"I don't *believe* it!" Traci cried shrilly.

Chapter 8

Brenda pulled herself up and craned her neck to see what Traci was staring at. The booths along the back wall were all filled. In one booth, an elderly couple were sharing an enormous banana split. In the next booth, a mother was reaching across the table with a napkin, trying to wipe the chocolate smears off a little boy's chin.

When Brenda saw the couple in the corner booth, she cried out, too.

She could see only the back of the girl's head. But she recognized Halley's disheveled blonde hair at once.

She could see the boy's smiling face clearly.

Halley and Noah.

They had tall soda glasses in front of them. They were holding hands across the table.

Noah had a goofy, dreamy look on his chubby face.

"I don't *believe* it!" Traci cried again, her voice rising over the distorted electric guitars from the jukebox.

"Traci — what are you *doing*?" Brenda cried.

But before Brenda could stop her, Traci had slid out of the booth and was making her way quickly toward the corner booth, her hands clenched into tight fists at her sides.

Oh, wow, Brenda thought unhappily. *I guess I should've warned Traci. About Halley and Noah. But I didn't know. I really didn't know they were actually seeing each other.*

Brenda pushed herself up from the booth and reluctantly followed Traci.

Does this mean that Halley has forgotten about Ted? Brenda wondered.

Why is she only interested in my boyfriend and my friend's boyfriend?

Doesn't she realize how sick that is? Doesn't she care?

By the time Brenda reached the corner booth, Noah's face was bright red. He was holding up both hands as if trying to shield himself from Traci's wrath.

"I was going to call you!" he was shouting. "Really, Traci. I was going to call you."

Brenda turned to Halley, expecting her to

be embarrassed. After all, here she was, sneaking out with Traci's boyfriend.

But, to Brenda's surprise, Halley's features were drawn tight in anger.

Traci, her silvery eyes wild with fury, tossed her black hair behind her head. "I don't believe this, Halley," she cried, turning away from Noah. "I don't believe that you — "

"Whoa!" Halley said calmly, raising one hand in a stop signal. "What's your problem, Traci?"

"Huh? My p-problem?" Traci sputtered. "My problem is that you are sitting here, holding hands with Noah, and — and — he's my boyfriend!" Traci blurted out, her hands flying up in the air.

Brenda lingered a few feet back. She saw that the old couple had put down their spoons and were staring at this angry drama in the corner booth.

"I didn't *force* Noah to come here with me," Halley said smugly.

"I was going to call you," Noah repeated, his face still bright red.

"It's not like you *own* him," Halley told Traci.

Traci opened her mouth wide to reply, but no sound came out.

Standing behind Traci, Brenda shoved her hands into her jeans pockets, feeling really embarrassed. Half the restaurant was staring at them now.

"I really was going to call you," Noah said.

"That's so lame," Traci told him, rolling her eyes. "Don't ever call me again, Noah."

She flashed Halley a dirty look, then spun around and stormed back to the booth. Dropping a five-dollar bill on the table with a trembling hand, she grabbed up her jacket and headed quickly for the exit.

Brenda hurried after her. "Traci — wait up!"

A few seconds later, they were out in the parking lot, walking quickly toward Traci's car. "Wait up!" Brenda repeated, lowering her head against the cold, gusting wind.

The sky was gray and starless. The wind carried cold drops of rainwater. Somewhere in the far distance, thunder rumbled.

"I wanted to pour that soda over her head," Traci said through clenched teeth. "I really did."

"First Ted, then Noah," Brenda said wistfully, jogging to catch up with her friend.

Traci turned to face Brenda at the car. "Your cousin really is messed up," she said heatedly, the pale parking lot lights reflecting the anger in her eyes.

"Tell me about it," Brenda replied bitterly,

thinking of the words smeared in blood on her bedroom wall.

"You have to get rid of her. You really do," Traci said, breathing hard, her breath steaming up in front of her.

"What can I do?" Brenda replied. "My mom told me her parents' court hearing was put off for three months. That means Halley will be staying with us all winter."

Traci unlocked the car door with a trembling hand. She pulled open the door, then raised her eyes to Brenda's. "Did I act like a total jerk in the restaurant?"

Brenda shook her head. "No way, Traci. Halley is the total jerk."

"Don't leave out Noah," Traci said bitterly.

"They're both total jerks," Brenda replied.

"Who *needs* him?" Traci declared, but her trembling voice revealed how upset she was.

She drove Brenda home in silence. "Call you later, maybe," she said.

"Yeah. Later," Brenda told her. She slammed the car door and, lowering her head against the cold drizzle of rain, began to run up the driveway. Traci's tires squealed over the damp pavement as she roared away.

Brenda was nearly to the front stoop when she realized her little blue Geo was gone. She stopped short and stared at the empty driveway.

Has it been stolen? she wondered.

The front door swung open. Her father appeared in a square of yellow light from the hallway. "I thought I heard someone out here," he said.

"Dad — my car!" Brenda cried, pointing to the dark, empty driveway.

"Halley took it," he told her, holding open the glass storm door, motioning for her to get inside. "Come in, Brenda. It's raining."

Shivering, Brenda stepped past him into the brightness of the hallway. "What do you *mean*, 'Halley took it'?"

Mr. Morgan helped her tug off her jacket.

"She borrowed it," her mother said, appearing in the living room doorway, a mug of tea in her hand.

"Huh?" Brenda reacted with surprise.

"She said you said it was okay," Mrs. Morgan said.

"But that was *last* night — " Brenda protested. "I really didn't — "

"Brenda," Mr. Morgan cut in sharply, "I hope you're not going to make a scene about this. After last night . . ."

"What about last night?" Brenda snapped.

"You weren't using the car," Mrs. Morgan said, "and Halley needed it. So I didn't see any harm in letting her take it." She frowned. "Brenda, it's not like you to be selfish."

"You're really not being nice to your cousin," Mr. Morgan added, staring hard at Brenda. He had a pudgy, round face with thinning red hair on top, and the same penetrating green eyes as Brenda's.

Brenda began to sputter a reply, but caught herself. "I — I have to go upstairs and change," she said. "I'm really chilled."

"Halley said she'd bring the car back early," Mrs. Morgan called as Brenda started up the stairs. "She just had a study date."

"I know. I saw her," Brenda muttered.

"Brenda, wait," her father called.

Brenda stopped and turned around halfway up the stairs.

"I have an apology to make," he said, his expression troubled as he stared up at her. He suddenly looked much older to Brenda. She felt a pang of sadness, seeing the age lines at the corners of his eyes, the gray among the red, thinning hair.

"The guy who was supposed to come today," her father said. "You know. To remove the wallpaper and paint your room. He didn't show up. He's coming tomorrow. He promised me."

"You mean — " Brenda started, her throat catching.

"The words. They're still there," Mr. Morgan said regretfully. "If you would rather sleep downstairs on the couch tonight, I'd understand."

"I still think you should've called the police," Mrs. Morgan cut in, holding the steaming mug of tea in both hands. "Someone definitely broke into this house and vandalized Brenda's room."

Brenda sighed. She didn't feel like starting this argument all over again. "I'll sleep in my room. It's okay," she said and hurried up the rest of the stairs.

"Oh, by the way — Ted called," her mother said.

Brenda turned again. "What did you say to him?"

"Shhh. You'll wake up your brother," Mrs. Morgan scolded, raising a finger to her lips.

"What did you say to Ted?" Brenda demanded.

"Just that you were out," her mother replied defensively. "That's all. What was I *supposed* to say?"

"That's fine," Brenda told her and made her way to her room.

The ugly, scrawled words greeted her as she clicked on the ceiling light. They had faded to a dark brown.

Forcing herself to look away, Brenda changed into a long, flannel nightshirt, tossing her clothes onto the chair by the closet.

The jack-o'-lantern they had carved the night before grinned at her from a corner of her desk. It reminded her of her Halloween party.

I've got to get busy on it, Brenda thought. It's less than two weeks away, and I haven't done a thing.

She thought of giving Ted a call, but changed her mind. Maybe she'd see him in school tomorrow.

Am I still furious at him? she asked herself.

She couldn't decide.

She made her way downstairs and pulled a can of Coke from the refrigerator. Then she returned to her room to do some homework.

She heard Halley come in about an hour later. Voices downstairs. Her father laughing. Halley talking excitedly.

Brenda quickly closed her door.

I certainly don't want to see Halley again tonight, she thought.

She yawned and glanced at the clock. A few minutes past eleven. She decided to go to bed.

She turned out the light. Then, as she pulled down the covers, the jack-o'-lantern on the desk across the room caught her eye. In the gray light from the bedroom window, it grinned at her.

An evil grin, Brenda decided.

A very evil grin.

She shuddered. "You're not going to grin at me like that all night," she said aloud.

Padding barefoot across the shag rug, Brenda grabbed the pumpkin with both hands and turned it until it faced the wall. Then she crept back to bed and pulled the covers up to her chin.

Outside the window, the wind howled, sending sheets of rain pattering against the glass. A flash of jagged lightning cast the room in a brief, silvery glow.

The scrawled letters on the wall seemed to pop out at her, then quickly fade as the lightning faded.

Brenda closed her eyes, shutting out the ugly wall.

She thought about Ted. She tried to remember all the fun times they'd had. But her mind kept bringing back the picture of him in the car, Halley's blonde hair over his face as they kissed in her driveway.

I'll never forgive you, Ted, she thought.

Or maybe I will. I don't know.

I've got to get to sleep, she told herself, propping up the pillows and sliding onto her back.

I'll be a wreck tomorrow. I really have to turn off my mind so I can fall asleep.

She forced her eyes closed. But a loud crack of thunder startled them open again.

Got to get to sleep. Got to get to sleep.

Something across the room caught her eye. Something *moved*.

She raised her head on the pillow, squinting into the darkness.

And as she stared, she saw it move. The pumpkin. It began to turn.

Brenda stared in wide-eyed horror as the pumpkin, half in shadow, half in gray light from the window, slowly turned.

As its face rotated into view, its sharply cut features began to glow. The triangular eyes, the crooked nose, the jagged, toothsome grin — all glowed orange-yellow, as if an invisible candle had been lit inside.

"Nooo!" Brenda cried in a choked whisper.

The jack-o'-lantern grinned at her, glowing eerily. And as Brenda stared, the wide mouth began to move.

The crooked teeth lowered themselves as the mouth pulled itself shut.

The eyes began to spin, slowly at first, then rapidly until they were a bright, whirling, yellow glow.

"Nooo!" Brenda cried again. Her voice sounded tiny and childlike.

"Noooo! Please!"

The jack-o'-lantern's mouth closed, making a disgusting, wet sucking sound. Then opened. Then closed again as the eyes whirled madly, staring blindly across the room at Brenda.

And then, as the hideous, jagged lips continued to move, the wet sucking sound growing louder, Brenda heard the jack-o'-lantern's voice, dry as wind, dry as death.

The grin widened. The yellow eyes whirled. The mouth opened and closed.

And the jack-o'-lantern rasped: *"SEE YOU ON HALLOWEEN."*

Chapter 9

"Nooo!" Brenda's wail rose through the dark room like a siren.

She sat straight up in bed, her heart pounding.

She could feel the hot beads of perspiration on her forehead.

Staring in fright through the gray darkness, she saw that the pumpkin had turned back to the wall.

No.

It hadn't turned back, she slowly realized. It had never turned.

A dream. An ugly nightmare, as ugly as the scrawled words covered in shadow on her wall. As ugly as the jack-o'-lantern's grin.

All just a nightmare.

She wiped her forehead with the sleeve of her nightshirt.

And why shouldn't she have nightmares?

Halley was making her life a complete nightmare.

Brenda stared hard at the pumpkin, assuring herself that it had never really lit up, never uttered that whispered threat. Then she let her head sink back to the pillow and fell into a deep, dreamless sleep.

"We still have a date to the Homecoming dance," Ted said.

"Huh?" Brenda's reaction was surprise mixed with anger. "Are you kidding me?"

She had started to walk home from school the next afternoon, a sunny but brisk day with white, fleecy clouds high in the sky. Crossing Oakridge Street in front of the high school, she had caught a glimpse of him in the corner of her eye.

He was loping after her, his long legs making their storklike motions, his brown hair bobbing in the wind, his backpack slung over one broad shoulder. "Hey, Brenda — whoa!" he had called.

Pretending not to hear him, she had kept up her steady pace, waving to some kids she knew who rumbled past in a big red Taurus stationwagon.

Ted had caught up easily and grabbed her arm. Then, before she could pull free, he had made his surprising announcement that they still had a date for Friday night. Surprising since she hadn't talked to him since . . . since seeing him with Halley that afternoon.

"What makes you think I'd go with you?" she asked angrily.

He shrugged and crinkled his eyes at her, giving her his best boyish smile. "I just thought you might want to," he said quietly. "Listen, Brenda, I'm really sorry. I've been calling you for days, you know. And every time, you just hang up."

"You're sorry? About what?" she demanded, continuing to walk. The wind shifted, and she could hear the blare of the marching band from the practice field beside the school.

"About . . . you know," Ted replied, blushing. He swept a hand back through his thick, brown hair.

Brenda stopped walking and turned to him, her eyes searching his. "Halley broke up with you? Is that it? She's going with Noah now, so you decide you'll come back to me. Your second choice."

His eyes widened in surprise. "Huh? Noah? What about Noah?"

"Give me a break, Ted," Brenda said sharply. "This innocent act is really the pits."

"Halley is going out with Noah?" Ted repeated, pronouncing each word slowly and distinctly. His expression remained astonished. "Since when?"

Brenda continued to stare into his eyes. "You really didn't know that?"

"Really," he replied, shifting his backpack to the other shoulder. They started walking again, in silence, for half a block. A school bus squealed to a halt at a stop sign. Two boys about Randy's age chased a girl in a yellow windbreaker across the street, chanting her name — Priscilla — over and over.

"Your cousin Halley really gets around," Ted muttered, shaking his head.

"Tell me about it," Brenda replied, rolling her eyes.

"She's nice, though," he added, avoiding her eyes.

Brenda didn't reply.

As they stopped at the corner, he suddenly put his arm around her shoulders. She started to pull away, then decided not to.

She realized she was happy they were getting back together.

"I still really like you," Ted said, blushing.

"I like you, too," she whispered back, leaning her head against the broad shoulder of his silver-and-blue school jacket.

"I just think we should see other people,

too," he continued. "You know. Not be so serious."

The words stung Brenda, but she forced herself not to react.

He still likes Halley, she realized unhappily.

He still wants to go out with Halley.

Maybe he's only taking me to this stupid dance on Friday night because she wouldn't go with him.

"Did you ask Halley to the dance first?" The words burst out of her mouth in a strange, tight voice Brenda had never heard before.

He still had his arm around her shoulder. His eyes widened in surprise. "No way," he told her. "I asked you weeks ago, remember?"

The answer didn't satisfy her, but she decided not to pursue it.

He leaned his head down and kissed her. His lips were dry and scratchy against hers.

She returned the kiss, but Halley spoiled it, creeping into her thoughts. *Did he kiss Halley like this?*

Halley is spoiling everything, Brenda thought, ending the kiss and starting toward her home again. Everything.

If only she'd go away. Forever. We'd all be so happy. . . .

* * *

"So is Ted still hung up on Halley?" Traci asked, shoving the last chunk of a Milky Way bar into her mouth.

"Probably. I don't know," Brenda muttered, picking at a hangnail on the back of her thumb.

Traci had stayed for dinner — spaghetti and meatballs and a big tossed salad. Now they were up in Brenda's room, scarfing down little bite-sized Milky Way bars that were supposed to be saved for Halloween, and waiting for Dina to come from her job.

Brenda had taken the opportunity to tell Traci about how she and Ted had made up. Sort of. Traci reacted to the news with suspicion. "Halley wants them both," she said bitterly. "You can bet on it."

"Maybe," Brenda replied wistfully. "Anyway, I guess I'll go with Ted Friday night. It's our last Homecoming dance, after all."

Traci sighed and didn't reply.

Brenda felt a stab of remorse. Traci still hadn't gotten over the shock of seeing Noah with Halley.

"So where is the lovely Halley Benson tonight?" Traci asked sarcastically. "Out scouting more of the local talent?"

Brenda shrugged. "I have no idea where she is. I barely speak to her anymore."

"Does she care?" Traci asked, tearing open another candy bar.

"Not much," Brenda replied. "As long as she can borrow my car whenever she wants."

She started to say more, but Dina's voice suddenly burst into the room. "Hey, guys, I can hear every word you're saying."

It took Brenda a moment to realize that Dina's voice was coming from the air vent. "Come upstairs," she shouted into the vent on the floor.

"Really. You can stand in the hall down here and hear every word," Dina called up. "Good thing you weren't gossiping about me!"

"We were just going to start!" Traci joked.

Dina appeared in the bedroom doorway a few seconds later, looking tired and even more pale than usual. "What did you do to your hair?" Traci asked.

The question caught Dina by surprise. "Nothing. I haven't had time to wash it."

Brenda laughed. "Traci sure knows how to make with the compliments, doesn't she?"

"Give me a break," Traci replied. She tossed a candy bar to Dina. Dina caught it in one hand, then let her backpack slide off her shoulder onto Brenda's bed. She was wearing loose-fitting gray sweats.

"Are we ready to kill Halley?" Dina asked,

dropping down onto the shag rug, leaning her back against the bed.

"I know *I* am!" Traci exclaimed unhappily.

"Wait. Let me get a pad," Brenda said, crossing the room to the desk. She glanced at the jack-o'-lantern, its face still toward the wall. "We've got to get serious about this murder," Brenda said, pulling a long writing pad from the desk drawer. "We have to turn it in in a week."

"I have some good ideas," Traci announced, reaching for another Milky Way. "I've been thinking about murdering Halley a lot. In fact, I've been thinking about nothing *but!*"

Brenda laughed. "At least you've kept your sense of humor."

"Who's kidding?" Traci joked.

Mrs. Morgan's voice through the air vent interrupted them. "Brenda, your dad and I are going out. Just to the Smithsons' for a few hours. Watch Randy, okay?"

"Okay," Brenda called down. She turned to her friends. "Good. Now we can go downstairs and do our plotting in the living room. It's much more comfortable than this cramped little closet."

"At least you've got nice white walls now," Dina said as they collected their things and headed for the stairs.

"Yeah. The guy came and did everything," Brenda said, glancing at the wall where the bloody words had been scrawled. "Now it's just like new."

Except, that in her mind, she could still see the ugly words. And probably always would.

They settled in the living room, Brenda and Traci on the couch, Dina in the big armchair across from it. Dina pulled off her sneakers and turned sideways in the big, old chair, her long legs hanging over one padded chair arm.

"So? What are your ideas?" Brenda asked Traci. "How does Halley get it?"

Traci snickered. She raised her hands and squeezed them together as if she were choking someone.

"She gets strangled?" Brenda cried. "I love it!"

Traci shook her head. "No. Forget strangling. It's too good for her."

"Maybe we should hang her," Brenda suggested. "We could have her tied up and — "

"I think we should change our victim's name," Dina interrupted, frowning. "You and Traci are taking this too seriously. You're starting to scare me."

Traci laughed. "You think we really want to murder Halley?"

Dina nodded. "Yeah. You're giving me the creeps."

"Let's stick with stabbing," Traci said, changing the subject back. "It's a Halloween party, see. Everyone is in costume."

"Right," Brenda agreed, writing quickly on the pad. "Halley is in her gorilla costume. I'm a clown. Dina's a monk. And" — she raised her eyes to Traci — "what's your costume going to be?"

"A peacock," Traci revealed, grinning. Brenda and Dina reacted with surprise. "I got these great peacock feathers," Traci explained, her eyes lighting up. "And I've made this great-looking peacock tail. I found a bird mask in a store. And I'm going to sew — "

Dina groaned. "You and Brenda are so creative. You really make me sick."

"Okay. Okay. So you're a peacock," Brenda said impatiently, scribbling on the notepad. "Let's stick to our murder. Which one of us gets to stab Halley?"

"Mrs. Ryland said it should be the least likely suspect," Dina recalled. "It should be the person you'd never suspect."

"Well, I guess that's *you*," Brenda told Dina. "I mean, Traci and I have good reasons for hating Halley. But you don't. So you should be the murderer."

Dina reached up and scratched the bottom of her foot through the white sock. "Yaaay!" she cheered. "I'm a murderer!"

"But we have to make it tricky," Traci said thoughtfully. "We have to — "

"I need a Coke or something," Dina interrupted, climbing to her feet. "Can I get anybody anything?"

"Bring three Cokes," Brenda said.

Dina disappeared toward the kitchen. The front door opened, startling Brenda and Traci. Halley entered and wiped her sneakers on the mat. "Hi, guys," she called, poking her head into the living room. Without waiting for a reply, she turned and hurried up the stairs.

A few minutes later, Dina returned, and Traci continued telling her plot idea. "We're at the costume party," she began, "and Dina convinces Brenda to switch costumes with her."

"Huh?" Brenda sat up straight, the pen poised over the pad.

"Dina takes the clown costume, and you put on the monk costume," Traci explained to Brenda.

"Why would she do that?" Brenda demanded.

"I get it," Dina said, taking a noisy sip from the soda can. "So when the clown stabs Halley, everyone thinks the murderer is Brenda."

"Right!" Traci cried, grinning. "See, Brenda. Everyone knows that you're the clown. So when Dina stabs Halley wearing the clown costume, everyone in the room is convinced that you murdered her. No one knows that Dina switched costumes with you."

"Pretty good!" Dina exclaimed.

Brenda tugged at a strand of copper-colored hair, staring down fretfully at the writing pad. "Hmmm . . . I don't know, Traci."

"It's real tricky, don't you think?" Traci insisted.

"But then what happens when I pull back my monk's hood?" Brenda asked, nibbling on the end of her pen. "Everyone will know that it *wasn't* me. And then I'd tell everyone that Dina was wearing my costume. And the whole thing would be over."

"Well . . ." Traci twisted her face in a thoughtful pose. "Maybe Dina has to kill you, too. So you don't reveal the secret."

"A double murder!" Dina exclaimed. "Maybe Mrs. Ryland will give us extra credit!"

Brenda and Traci laughed.

"She won't give us any credit at all if we don't come up with a perfect murder," Brenda said.

"I'm hungry! Is there anything to eat?" Randy appeared in the doorway, a pitiful expression on his face.

"I'm kind of hungry, too," Dina admitted.

"I think there's some chocolate cake in the kitchen," Brenda said, climbing to her feet. She tossed the pad and pen onto the couch. "Let's check it out."

That ended the murder plotting session. After their cake, Randy went into the den to watch TV. Traci and Dina decided they had to get home to do other homework.

"We're making progress, I think," Brenda said, seeing them to the front door.

"Plotting a murder is harder than I thought," Traci said.

Dina giggled. "I'm glad it isn't something we have to do every day!"

Brenda closed the door behind them. Thinking about the murder plot, she returned to the kitchen and cleaned up.

Maybe Dina should switch costumes without telling anyone, she thought. Then there wouldn't be any witness to squeal on her.

Then she thought: *I* should be the killer — not Dina. *I'm* the one who should murder Halley. She's *my* cousin, after all.

The thought struck Brenda funny. She was chuckling about it as she climbed the stairs to her room. Upstairs, she saw that Halley had her door closed.

What's she doing in there? Brenda wondered bitterly. Planning whose boyfriend she's going to steal next? A strange picture flashed into Brenda's mind. In it, she saw Halley sitting on her bed, grasping a little doll in one hand. It was a Brenda doll, and Halley was gleefully pushing long pins into it.

I really hate her, Brenda thought, staring at the closed bedroom door. I really hate her, and she's going to live here in my house forever!

Trying to shake these depressing thoughts from her mind, Brenda made her way to her room, pulled out her government text, and dropped it onto her desk. Peering out the window, she saw the glare of headlights down below. She heard a car door slam, then another.

Her parents were home.

Good, she thought. They can get Randy to bed.

She lowered herself behind her desk — and realized with a jolt that the jack-o'-lantern was glowing.

"Oh!" A cry of surprise escaped her lips.

It grinned at her, flickering orange-yellow light behind its jagged smile. The triangular eyes appeared to gleam brightly into hers.

"Who lit this thing?" Brenda cried aloud.

And then the sour aroma filled her nostrils.

Her breath caught in her throat.

What is that awful smell?

Cautiously, she inhaled. It smelled like rotten meat.

Her stomach churned.

It must be the insides of the pumpkin.

But a pumpkin couldn't smell this bad — could it?

The foul odor lingered in her nose.

Holding her breath, Brenda reached for the pumpkin top with a trembling hand. Grasping the short stub of the stem, she pulled off the lid and peered inside.

"Nooooo!" The cry of horror burst from her lips without her realizing it.

The fetid odor rose up, encircled her, thick and foul.

The short candle in the center of the pumpkin glowed brightly, the yellow flame tilting from side to side.

And beside the candle lay a small, dark form.

"Ohhhhhh," Brenda moaned as her eyes focused on it and she realized it was the body of a bird.

A headless bird. Its head cut cleanly off, tendons and blood vessels poking through the open cavity of its neck.

The bird's body lay smouldering, stinking, beside the low candle.

Brenda swallowed hard, struggling to hold back the wave of nausea that swept over her.

"Noooo!"

As she started to back away from the ghastly sight, something else caught her attention. Something beside the bird.

Staring hard, Brenda saw that it was a folded-up piece of paper. A note?

Her hand shook as she carefully reached inside the pumpkin. Careful not to touch the putrid corpse, her fingers wrapped around the paper and pulled it out.

The foul smell overwhelmed her. She started to gag.

The waves of nausea rolled up from her stomach, one after the other.

Somehow she managed to unfold the paper and read the dark, scrawled words: YOU'RE NEXT. ON HALLOWEEN.

Then, with a moan of surrender, she leaned over her desk and started to vomit.

Chapter 10

"Brenda? Brenda — are you okay?"

Brenda's parents burst into the room a few moments later, followed by Halley and Randy.

"I — uh — I — " Brenda's shoulders heaved. She pointed to the still-glowing pumpkin. "It's so awful."

"Ugh. What's that smell?" Mrs. Morgan demanded, holding her fingers over her nose.

"Blow out the candle," Mr. Morgan instructed Halley.

Halley moved reluctantly to obey. Mrs. Morgan put an arm around Brenda's quaking shoulders. "Let's get you cleaned up."

"Halley did it!" Brenda shrieked, pointing an accusing finger at her cousin.

Halley's eyes grew wide with surprise. She took a step back from the desk, as if pushed back by the force of Brenda's accusation.

"Halley put it in there! She's — she's trying

to drive me crazy!" Brenda screamed, out of control.

"I did not!" Halley protested angrily, tossing her hair behind the shoulders of her red sweater. "I don't even know what it is!"

"She did it!" Brenda accused as her mother struggled to lead her out of the room.

"Brenda — stop," her father said quietly. "Let's get everything cleaned up and get this disgusting pumpkin out of here. Then maybe we can talk. Calmly and rationally."

"No!" Brenda wailed. "No, we can't! Not while *she's* here!"

Her mother led her to the bathroom to get her cleaned up. "Randy — go get the sponge mop and bucket in the kitchen," Brenda heard her father say.

"Why can't Brenda do it?" she heard her brother whine. "*She* made the mess!"

"I really don't know why Brenda is accusing me," Halley said coldly, her blue eyes glaring across the table at Brenda.

They were all seated at the kitchen table, under the bright cone of white light from the low ceiling fixture above their heads. Mr. and Mrs. Morgan were next to each other at one end, Randy sat eating a bowl of Frosted Flakes at the other. Brenda, her hands wrapped around a mug of hot tea, avoided Halley's stare from across the table.

"I wasn't even in Brenda's room," Halley continued shrilly. "I never go in Brenda's room. I don't go where I'm not wanted."

Brenda frowned down at her tea and didn't reply.

"Well, *somebody* is vandalizing Brenda's room," Mr. Morgan said quietly, his hands clasped together on the table. "These acts of vandalism aren't being done by a ghost." He raised his eyes to Randy.

"Hey!" Randy cried, a white milk mustache above his lips. He dropped his spoon into the cereal bowl. "Don't look at *me!*"

"Are these your little jokes, Randy?" Mrs. Morgan asked, keeping her voice low and soft.

Both of her parents, Brenda realized, were trying to keep the discussion calm and under control. But Brenda could feel her heart pounding, the blood throbbing at her temples. She wanted to scream. She wanted to leap across the table and tear Halley's hair out.

"No way!" Randy was protesting. "No way, Mom! It wasn't me!"

"Someone must have broken in," Halley suggested. "Someone had to break in, through Brenda's window, maybe."

"That's impossible," Brenda muttered, still

not raising her eyes. She had a sour taste in her mouth. She didn't want to be sitting here, discussing this so calmly.

She wanted her parents to get tough with Halley, to force Halley to tell the truth.

"But who would do these things?" Mrs. Morgan asked. "Who would do such awful things to you, Bren? And why?"

Brenda shrugged. "Ask Halley," she replied bitterly.

"Stop accusing me!" Halley cried.

Mr. Morgan raised both hands. "Let's keep our voices down. Let's try to stay — "

"Just stop accusing me!" Halley screamed at Brenda.

"You did it! You did it!" Brenda screamed back, losing control.

"Brenda — stop!" Mr. Morgan yelled.

"Don't yell at me — yell at *her*!" Brenda wailed. She accidentally bumped the mug with her hand, sending tea splashing across the white Formica table.

Halley jumped to her feet, her blue eyes flashing angrily. "You've been so horrible to me, ever since I came here. You never gave me a chance, Brenda. What did I do to you? Huh? What did I ever do to you?" Tears formed in Halley's eyes and rolled down her pale cheeks.

"Don't listen to her!" Brenda desperately cried to her parents. "Don't listen to that! She's evil! I know you won't believe me — but Halley is evil!"

"I — I don't believe this! I want to go home!" Halley shrieked. She shoved her chair back so hard, it toppled over backwards. As it clattered loudly to the linoleum, Halley fled from the room, sobbing uncontrollably.

"She's evil! Evil!" Brenda shrieked.

"Brenda — stop!" Mr. Morgan demanded, standing up and putting a hand firmly on her trembling shoulder. "Stop. Get yourself together."

"Brenda, I expected so much more of you," her mother said through clenched teeth. "Halley is going through such a tough time. I can't believe your attitude toward her. It's sick, Brenda. It's really sick."

"Go to bed. Get some sleep," Brenda's father ordered.

"And tomorrow I want you to apologize to your cousin," Mrs. Morgan said sternly, shaking her head.

Avoiding her parents' eyes, Brenda climbed to her feet and stumbled out of the kitchen.

"Can I have more Frosted Flakes?" she heard Randy ask as she started up the stairs to her room.

* * *

"So did you apologize to Halley?" Dina asked.

Brenda had met her in the lunchroom at school the next afternoon, and they'd settled into a corner of the vast, noisy room to talk.

As they had pulled their sandwiches and yogurt containers from their lunchbags, Brenda had related the unpleasant events of the night before. As she told Dina the story, she found herself growing even angrier.

"No, I didn't apologize," she shouted at Dina. "No way I'll ever apologize to her."

"Whoa. Calm down," Dina said, a little surprised by Brenda's emotional reaction. "You can't let her get to you, Bren."

"I — I can't help it," Brenda replied, struggling to punch the little straw through the top of her juice box. "I — I just — "

"You look terrible," Dina interrupted. "Look at the dark rings around your eyes. You look like a raccoon." She ripped open a bag of potato chips. "You're letting her get to you, Bren. You're letting her win."

"You're not cheering me up," Brenda said sharply.

Dina pushed the bag of potato chips across the table to her. "Have some. Potato chips always cheer *me* up."

Brenda glanced down at the bag but didn't take any. "It — it's not just Halley, you know. It's my parents," she said, shaking her head sadly. "They just take Halley's side no matter what."

"Weird," Dina muttered through a mouthful of peanut butter and jelly.

"Halley smears blood on my wall and puts a disgusting dead bird in my room with a threatening note. And my parents say I'm not being understanding of her."

Dina swallowed a small section of her sandwich. "It's ridiculous," she agreed.

"It just isn't fair," Brenda continued bitterly. She still hadn't touched a bite of lunch. "How *can* I be understanding? Halley is a monster! A monster!"

Dina reached across the table and squeezed Brenda's hand. "Have some lunch. You'll feel better. Really."

Brenda moaned and rolled her eyes. "I'll never feel better. Not while Halley is in my house. You know, I never even told my parents about Halley and Ted. How she tried to steal my boyfriend! Can you *imagine*? Living in the same house and trying to steal my boyfriend!"

"But you and Ted are okay now, right?" Dina asked, her small, dark eyes studying Brenda's face.

Brenda started to reply when someone grabbed her shoulders from behind and cried, "Guess who?"

Startled, she spun around. "Ted!" she cried.

"Speak of the devil," Dina said, laughing.

Ted lowered his gaze to Dina. "You were talking about me?"

"Don't get a swelled head," Brenda told him. "We weren't saying anything nice."

Ted leaned over Brenda to reach for Dina's potato chip bag. He grabbed a handful of chips and stuffed them into his mouth. "Can I have some chips?" he asked Dina, crunching loudly.

"No," she joked. "Give those back."

He opened his mouth so she could see the chewed-up chips. "Here."

"You're so gross," Brenda complained.

"I've got to go," Dina said, jamming what was left of her sandwich into the brown lunchbag. "I'll come over later, okay, Bren?"

"Yeah. Good," Brenda told her. "I have to work on my government paper. But come anyway."

"Thanks for the chips," Ted said. He finished off the bag, crinkled it up, and tossed it onto the table.

"Any time," Dina told him. "Bye." She headed toward the exit.

"She's so tall," Ted said, pulling back the

chair beside Brenda and lowering himself over the chairback. "She should try out for basketball."

"She hates basketball," Brenda told him, making a face. "And don't ever say anything like that to Dina. She's terribly sensitive about her height."

"What will she do if I call her Beanpole?" Ted asked, opening Brenda's yogurt container. "What flavor is this? You want it?"

"You can have it," Brenda said with a sigh. "I'm not very hungry. I — "

Her voice trailed off because she suddenly realized Ted wasn't listening. He was staring at something across the room.

"Ted?"

What was he staring at so intently?

Following his gaze, she saw what had grabbed Ted's attention. Halley had entered the lunchroom, snuggling against Noah. Noah, she saw, had his arm around Halley's shoulders. Halley leaned her head against his chest as they walked.

What a touching scene, Brenda thought sarcastically.

She returned her gaze to Ted and felt a cold shudder run down her back. As he watched Halley cling so closely to Noah, Ted had the strangest expression on his face.

An expression Brenda had never seen before.

Sadness and envy and anger all mixed together.

That evening after dinner, Brenda was leaning over the keyboard, staring at the amber screen of her computer monitor. She was trying to make some progress on the government paper.

Randy had interrupted twice, begging her to come and see how he'd made it to the tenth level of some new Super Nintendo game. She'd finally had to shut the bedroom door to keep him out.

She tried to concentrate on the powers of the Supreme Court, but her mind kept wandering. When Dina's voice behind her called, "How's it going?" Brenda nearly jumped out of her chair.

"Sorry," Dina apologized, pulling off her leopardskin-style jacket. "Didn't mean to scare you. Your mom let me in."

"I thought you were Randy," Brenda said. She sighed. "I'm not getting too far with this paper."

Dina was wearing straight-legged black jeans and an oversized green cotton turtleneck sweater. She stepped up behind Brenda and studied the monitor screen. "Well, you spelled your name right at the top. That's a good start."

"Thanks for your support," Brenda replied dryly.

"How'd it go with Ted at lunch? Are you two okay now?" Dina asked, backing up to the bed and dropping down onto it.

Brenda spun her chair around to face the bed. "I don't know. I guess we're okay. It's not like before, though. Ted and I — we're not real comfortable with each other. And I caught him staring at Halley and Noah with the weirdest look on his face."

"Uh-oh," Dina muttered. "You're still going to the Homecoming thing with him?"

"Yeah. I guess." Brenda shrugged.

"Speaking of Noah, where's Traci tonight?" Dina asked, drawing patterns with her finger on Brenda's bedspread. "Is she coming over? Are we going to work on our murder?"

Brenda shook her head. "Traci had to go somewhere with her parents. To some cousin's house or something. She can't come."

"Traci has a million cousins," Dina said wistfully. "I wish I had a big family."

The remark surprised Brenda. "You do? How come?"

"Well, it gets kind of lonely, just Mom and

me," Dina replied, staring out the window at the darkening night. "After the divorce, all of Dad's relatives just kind of dropped us. As if we weren't part of the family anymore. As if we just didn't exist. It was weird."

"I guess," Brenda replied awkwardly. And then she added, "You can have *my* cousin if you want!"

Dina snickered. "No thanks. You keep her."

As if on cue, Halley appeared in the doorway. "Brenda!" she cried, her features twisted in alarm, her hands gripping the sides of her hair. She burst into the room.

"Brenda!" she repeated in a tight, frightened voice. "I'm so sorry! There's been a horrible accident! A horrible accident!"

Chapter 11

Down the stairs. Out through the open front door.

Brenda followed Halley, her heart pounding, Halley's frightened voice echoing in her ears.

Where is she taking me? Why are we running outside like this? Brenda wondered.

Into a cold, clear night. The shock of the cold against her thin T-shirt made Brenda shudder. Goosebumps climbed her bare arms.

The front porchlight was on, casting a triangle of pale yellow light toward the driveway. Brenda could hear footsteps behind her. Dina, following in silence.

"Halley — what is it? Where?" Brenda's voice so shrill, so tiny.

Darkness encircled them. The wind tried to push Brenda back.

Halley stopped suddenly at the edge of the drive. Her hands rose to her face.

Brenda saw the car. Her car. Her prized Geo.

The passenger side was pushed in. Brenda

suddenly pictured a crushed soda can.

The windows were shattered. The door appeared to be bent in half.

"It wasn't my fault!" Halley told her in a trembling voice, her hands still pressed against her face. Her blonde hair ruffled wildly in the gusting wind, rising and falling about her head.

"Huh?" Brenda gaped in horror at her car. All crunched. All crunched and shattered and bent.

"I didn't see the stop sign," Halley told her, keeping her distance. "I — I don't know this neighborhood very well. The stop sign was kind of hidden."

Brenda couldn't take her eyes off the car. "You — you went through a stop sign?"

"But it wasn't my fault!" Halley cried. "The other car — it shouldn't have been going so fast. If it had been going slower, then it could have stopped. So you see — "

Something snapped inside Brenda.

If only Halley had apologized.

If only she hadn't made this stupid excuse.

If only she had STOPPED!

The blue car appeared to flame up in Brenda's mind. The dark sky flared red. The driveway became a molten red river. The ground glowed bright red.

And then everything went white.

Brenda closed her eyes. It was all too bright. Too frightening.

And when she opened them, Halley was still talking, still saying it wasn't her fault.

And Brenda opened her mouth and let out a hideous roar of anger.

And before she even realized she was moving, she had leapt at Halley, and her hands wrapped around Halley's throat.

And they were down on the cold, hard driveway, surrounded by blackness. All black now. Rolling in the shadows. Grunting and crying.

And the screams Brenda heard were far in the distance.

Was that Dina screaming, so far away?

Were Brenda's hands really pulling so hard at Halley's hair now?

Was Brenda really on top of Halley, trying to cut off her breath? Were they really rolling on the wet grass, over and over, their cries mingling with their groans of anger?

It wasn't real until the strong hands squeezed Brenda's shoulders.

It wasn't real until Brenda felt herself being pulled roughly away, being lifted up off her cousin, her hands thrashing wildly, her breath coming in short whimpers.

It was all red again. Blinding red. Throbbing red.

And then it was black.

And then she was staring into the pale porch-light, and Halley was still on her back on the grass.

And Brenda's father was holding her firmly, his hands locked on her quaking shoulders.

"What on earth? What on earth?" His words repeated in a frantic chant in her ear.

And her mother was screaming.

And Randy looked so thin and confused, hunched at the edge of the driveway, shivering, with his arms crossed in front of his slender chest.

And everyone was screaming and crying.

"It wasn't my fault! It wasn't my fault!"

Halley repeating her high-pitched refrain. "It was an accident! Just an accident! It wasn't my fault!"

Mrs. Morgan helping Halley to her feet. Brushing the wet grass and dirt off Halley's jacket.

"It wasn't my fault!" Halley's face all mud-stained.

Of course it wasn't an accident!

You did it, Halley! You did it to my car!

And suddenly, the fight was over. The energy was gone. Brenda surrendered to the weariness of her muscles, the overload of her brain.

Her shoulders slumped. Her head drooped.

"Brenda — are you finished? Can I let go now?" Mr. Morgan asked, his mouth right behind her ear, his hands holding her in their firm grip. "Is it over, Brenda? Can you control yourself now?"

"Yes." A whispered reply.

She shivered. It was so cold and dark.

She stared at her car. A crushed soda can.

"Brenda, are you calm? Are you finished?"

"Yes."

"It was just an accident," Mrs. Morgan said, her arm around Halley's shoulders.

Why is she hugging Halley and not me? Brenda wondered.

"It was just an accident, Brenda," her mother repeated, eyeing her so coldly. "We should be grateful that Halley wasn't hurt."

Brenda caught a flash in Halley's eyes. It was there for less than a second, but Brenda caught it. A gleam of triumph. Of victory.

"I don't understand you, Brenda," Mrs. Morgan scolded. "Halley is okay. That's the main thing."

I'll kill her, Brenda decided, gasping in the cold, wet air, her chest still heaving, her head throbbing.

I'll kill her for real.

I really will.

Chapter 12

Dina, her hair still wet from the shower, called Traci before school the next morning. Cradling the phone under her chin, she hunted for her sneakers under the bed as she waited for Traci to answer the phone.

"Hello?" Traci's voice was still hoarse from sleep.

"Traci? It's me."

"Dina? What time is it? I'm running a little late this morning," Traci said. She cleared her throat loudly. "Wish I could get back into bed."

"You don't want to miss Mr. Friedman's surprise quiz, do you?" Dina asked. She located one sneaker, but there was no trace of the second one.

"He has a surprise quiz every day," Traci groaned. "Big deal." Dina could hear Traci's mother in the background, yelling something. "I *know*, Mom!" Traci shouted. "Listen, Dina, what do you want? Everyone around here seems to be totally freaked this morning."

Dina hesitated. "I can only find one sneaker," she muttered, searching the cluttered closet floor.

"That's why you called?" Traci demanded impatiently. "Look — I haven't even brushed my teeth, and — "

"No," Dina interrupted. She spotted the sneaker on her desk chair, on top of a pile of dirty laundry. "I called because I'm really worried about Brenda."

Traci cleared her throat again. "Brenda? What's Brenda's problem?" And then she quickly added: "What did Halley do this time?"

"Wrecked her car," Dina said.

"Oh, wow," Traci moaned. "Not the Geo. Brenda loves that car."

"Halley practically totaled it," Dina told her friend, "and Brenda went psycho."

"She freaked?"

"She tried to strangle Halley in the driveway. It was horrible. The two of them were crying and wrestling around on the ground. I really think Brenda was trying to kill her."

"Oh, wow," Traci repeated. "That's bad."

"Mr. Morgan had to pull them apart," Dina reported.

"Is Brenda okay?" Traci asked.

"You mean is she hurt? No. She wasn't hurt. But I think she's really messed up." Dina's voice broke. "I'm so worried about her."

"She'll be even more messed up when I tell her what I saw yesterday afternoon," Traci revealed. And then she shouted: "I'll be off in one minute, Mom! Give me a break, okay?"

"Huh? Traci, what did you see? What are you talking about?" Dina demanded, standing in front of the dresser mirror and trying to brush her wet hair as she talked.

"I have to get off. My mom is having a cow!" Traci exclaimed.

"You *have* to tell me," Dina insisted.

Traci lowered her voice. "After school yesterday, I stayed late. I had some stuff to do in the computer lab. Anyway, I went out the back. You know. By the student parking lot. And I recognized the car parked in the corner back by the practice field. The only car still in the lot. It was Ted's red Honda."

"Yeah? So?" Dina asked impatiently. "So Ted stayed after school, too. Big deal."

"No. Wait," Traci whispered. "Ted was in the car. And guess who he was making out with?"

"Halley?"

"You won the prize," Traci replied dryly. "They were going at it like — *Coming, Mom! I'm hanging up now!*"

"But — but I thought Ted and Brenda were back together," Dina stammered.

"So does Brenda," Traci replied.

"I mean, they're going to the dance tomorrow night and everything. Maybe you shouldn't tell Brenda what you saw, Traci. She's so messed up already."

"Yeah. Maybe," Traci replied thoughtfully. "You're probably right, Dina. But do you *believe* Ted?"

"He and Halley deserve each other," Dina said bitterly.

"I was tempted to call Noah up and tell *him* about Ted and Halley," Traci revealed, snickering. "Noah is so dumb, he thinks Halley is only interested in him!"

"Halley sure is messing up a lot of people," Dina said thoughtfully.

Traci sighed. "I guess you and I will be home tomorrow night while everyone is at the dance. Stuffing ourselves with microwave popcorn and watching TV."

"I guess . . ." Dina replied softly.

"I've got to get off. I hear my mom on the steps," Traci whispered. "Bye." She hung up.

Dina replaced the receiver and carried her

sneakers over to the unmade bed. She glanced at the clock on the bedtable. Ten till eight. If she didn't hurry, she was going to be late.

She bent to pull on the left sneaker.

"Poor Brenda," she said aloud, shaking her head. "Poor Brenda."

Breakfast at Brenda's house was silent.

Silent as a tomb, Brenda thought, spooning up her Wheaties, gazing down at the cereal bowl to avoid her mother's disapproving stare.

"Your father took your car to the garage early," Mrs. Morgan said finally, as Brenda was finishing her cereal.

"Good," Brenda muttered, still avoiding her mother's eyes.

Halley had gotten up before everyone else and rushed off to school, probably so she wouldn't have to see Brenda or talk to anyone.

Randy had a bad sore throat. He was sleeping late. Maybe Mrs. Morgan would take him to school at lunchtime if he was feeling better.

So, breakfast was just Brenda and her mother, sitting in cold silence, avoiding each other.

Brenda's left elbow throbbed, and her entire right side ached and felt stiff. From the fight last night, she realized.

The fight.

She couldn't believe she had been in an actual fight. A fight with her own cousin.

Brenda sighed and pushed her chair away from the kitchen table. She'd never been in a fight in her life.

"I'm going now," she muttered. Her voice seemed to echo in the cold silence.

Maybe the fight was a good thing, Brenda thought, desperately trying to cheer herself up. Maybe now Halley will back off.

Brenda thought of her mangled car, the disgusting, headless bird, the blood-smeared threat on her wall — and her anger began to grow again.

These days, the anger never left, she realized sadly. The anger was always there, waiting, waiting in the pit of her stomach. Waiting to spread, to radiate through her entire body until she was choked by it, strangled by her own anger.

Ready to kill.

Kill Halley. Kill her — and *enjoy* it.

She stood up and started to the hallway to get her jacket. Turning at the kitchen doorway, she glanced back at her mother.

Mrs. Morgan stared at her coldly, then looked away.

* * *

All day in school, Brenda had the feeling that people were staring at her. Whispered conversations seemed to end when Brenda walked by. In class and in study hall, she had the feeling that eyes were burning into the back of her head.

Were kids talking about her? Had word about her fight with Halley spread so quickly around the school?

She wondered if Halley was telling everyone, making sure that everyone heard *her* side of it first.

I'd *love* to hear Halley's version of what happened, Brenda thought bitterly. I'll bet I know how she tells it: "I was in a terrible car accident, and my evil cousin Brenda attacked me before I even had a chance to recover from the shock."

Brenda had trouble concentrating all day. She kept watching for signs that people were gossiping about her. She had lunch with Ted, sitting across from him in a corner of the lunchroom.

Ted seemed nervous. Uncomfortable. He made a lot of jokes and kept talking really fast, which wasn't like him at all. His eyes darted around the crowded lunchroom. He kept tapping his hands on the tabletop as he ate.

Brenda told him about Halley smashing up

the blue Geo, but she didn't mention the fight.

"Was the car totaled? Can it be fixed?" he asked, taking the last bite of his ham sandwich and crumpling up the brown lunchbag in his big hands.

Brenda shrugged. "My dad took it to the garage this morning. I guess I'll find out later."

"Bummer," Ted muttered, glancing over her shoulder. "That was a neat car."

"Yeah. Bummer," Brenda repeated softly.

"We'll take my car to the dance," he offered. "Should I pick you up before the game, or do you want to meet at the stadium?"

"Pick me up," Brenda replied, tossing her apple across the aisle into a tall trash can. "Mom gives me an apple every day, and every day I throw it away."

"Well," Ted grinned, "you know what they say about an apple a day . . ."

"If the dance is a drag, we don't have to stay," Brenda told him.

The bell rang.

He jumped up quickly. She had the feeling he was glad their lunch was over, as if he were eager to get away.

Am I getting paranoid? she wondered.

I've been suspecting everyone all day. I keep feeling that everyone is talking about me and staring at me.

Am I cracking up?

"See you later, Bren," he said. He tossed his lunchbag in the trash and hurried from the lunchroom without waiting for her.

At home that evening, Brenda's mood didn't improve. Halley ate an early dinner by herself in the kitchen. Then she hurried upstairs to her room and slammed the door.

When Mr. Morgan got home from work, he announced that Brenda's car could be repaired. It would be expensive, but the insurance covered most of it.

"Will it be like new?" Brenda asked eagerly.

Mr. Morgan shook his head. "It'll look okay," he told Brenda, "but cars are really never quite the same after an accident."

Brenda nodded and took her place at the dinner table. Randy was over at a friend's down the block, so it was a quiet dinner. "It doesn't feel right without Randy here to complain about my meatloaf," Mrs. Morgan said with forced cheerfulness.

Nothing seemed right to Brenda. She had the feeling her parents had a lot of things they wanted to say to her, but were forcing themselves to hold it all in.

She excused herself early, having eaten a half-portion of the meatloaf and only a few

spoons of the mashed potatoes, and hurried upstairs to work on her government report.

Her parents started to talk rapidly in low
whispers as soon as Brenda left the room. She
knew they were talking about her.

Halley sure has done a good job of splitting
up this family, Brenda thought sadly. She sat
down at her desk, turned on the computer,
and began sifting through the notes for her
paper.

Traci and Dina came over later, a little after
eight-thirty, to talk about the murder plot.
Brenda was glad to see them at first. But her
mood darkened when she realized that Traci
and Dina were suddenly uncomfortable and
tense around her, too.

Again, Brenda had the feeling that they
weren't saying what was really on their minds,
that they were holding something back.

It must be my imagination, Brenda thought.

They tried to outline the murder plot step
by step, with Brenda typing it into the computer as they talked. But no one could concentrate. Traci kept going downstairs to get
drinks. Dina had to make several phone calls.
Brenda had to go help Randy, who had come
home after dinner, with several math problems
he couldn't figure out.

The three girls finally gave up. "We can finish it this weekend," Traci said. Brenda clicked off the computer, and they went down to the kitchen for a late snack.

Brenda was actually relieved when Traci and Dina left a little after ten. Everyone had been so tense!

Brenda's side still ached. She felt so sleepy, she could barely keep her eyes open. "I'm going to bed," she announced with a loud yawn to her startled parents.

"At ten o'clock? Are you sick?" her mother asked, glancing up from her book.

"Just tired," Brenda replied.

"Is Halley going to sleep, too?" Mrs. Morgan asked.

Brenda shrugged. "I don't know, Mom. I haven't seen her."

Mrs. Morgan shook her head and *tsk-tsked.* "She hasn't come out of her room all night. I think she's really upset."

Good! Brenda thought.

She didn't say anything. She was too tired to discuss Halley. Muttering good-night again, she turned and made her way, yawning, up to her room.

Brenda paused in front of Halley's bedroom. From the crack under the door, she could see that the light was still on inside. She wondered what Halley was doing.

Wearily, she walked the rest of the way down the hall to her room.

Tossing her clothes onto a chair, she slipped into a long, black-and-white-striped cotton nightshirt. She clicked off the overhead light, crept over the shag rug in the darkness, and eagerly slid under the covers.

It took only a few seconds to realize that something was wrong.

Brenda felt something damp on the back of her nightshirt.

Squirming, she felt another damp spot on her shoulder.

Something lumpy and wet.

What's going on? she wondered sleepily.

It took another few seconds to realize that something was in the bed. Something wet and bumpy beneath her.

"Ohh!" With a low cry of dread, she jerked upright, lowered her feet to the rug, and leapt up, shoving the covers away.

The dampness clung to her back.

She suddenly felt itchy all over.

What is it? What is it?

She lurched for the light switch. Her trembling hand fumbled against the dark wall until she found it. Clicking on the ceiling light, she blinked hard, forcing her eyes to adjust to the bright light.

And crept to her bed.

And saw the dark blobs on the sheet.

Still blinking, she realized at once what they were. Wet chunks of dark, raw meat.

She could smell them now. The putrid aroma invaded her nose.

Rotten meat. Chunks of it spread all over the sheet.

She had been lying on them.

And were they moving? Why did they appear to be moving?

No!

Staring hard, Brenda saw the tiny white worms crawling on the meat chunks. There were so many of them, the meat appeared to move.

Maggots!

Maggots in her bed.

Her back itched. She could still feel the dampness on the back of her nightshirt. Her entire body convulsed in a shudder of disgust.

Rotten meat crawling with maggots.

Brenda opened her mouth to scream. Then stopped.

"Oh. I know!" she cried aloud, staring at the crawling maggots.

"I know."

Yes. She understood now. She *knew*.

She knew what she had to do.

Chapter 13

The Homecoming dance was a lot more crowded than Brenda had expected. Maybe school dances are making a comeback, she thought, as Ted led her by the hand to the dance floor.

The gym was decorated with alternating rows of balloons, hundreds of balloons, all blue and silver, the McKinley High colors. A deejay had set up against one wall beneath a basketball hoop, and was sending out pulsating dance music with a CD player and a turntable.

The gym lights were low. The light bounced off the hundreds of balloons, making the room appear to shimmer and move, as if hundreds of fireflies were floating in the air. The music echoed off the tile walls, making the floor vibrate and hum.

It's like being inside a dark thunderstorm, Brenda thought, starting to dance with Ted.

Or maybe a tornado. Lightning flashing all around. The sound whirling on all sides.

Ted was a dark figure, moving in rhythm a few yards in front of her, one of several dark figures, shaking and moving inside the whirling storm.

It's so dark, Brenda thought. It feels so good.

I feel far away. Far away from everyone. Even though I'm here in this crowd in the middle of this vibrating, spinning storm.

McKinley had lost the football game 28–14. But the loss didn't seem to dampen anyone's spirits. Loud voices and laughter rose up over the steady, insistent pulsing of the music.

For a while, Brenda lost herself in the music. As Ted and the other dark figures continued to bend and move around her, she closed her eyes and floated happily, dreamily, thinking about nothing at all.

When a slow ballad replaced the pulsing dance music, she opened her eyes, expecting to see Ted hovering in front of her. But to Brenda's surprise, she was standing alone, couples gliding slowly around her.

She blinked, stunned. As if she had stepped from one dream into another.

And now everything seemed in slow motion. The music. The clinging couples dancing around her. The blink and shimmer of the lights on the rows of balloons. Her thoughts.

As if slowing the music had changed everything. Everything! And even deprived her of Ted.

Where was he?

Still in the old dream?

Brenda shook her head hard as if trying to clear it. A girl in a slinky black catsuit backed into her. "Oh. Sorry." Brenda's voice came out muffled against the loud horns and violins.

Violins?

I *am* in the wrong dream, she thought.

She made her way off the floor, dodging another couple, the strange lighting placing long shadows in Brenda's path as if trying to block her way.

"Hey, Ted?" She thought she saw him by the refreshment table. "Ted?"

No. It was another tall, broad-shouldered boy. He turned and grinned at her as she approached. "Hey, Brenda, how's it going?"

"Oh. Hi, Mark. You see Ted?" Her eyes searched the shadows, moving quickly over the dance floor.

"Ted? Huh-uh. Want a brownie or something?"

Brownies? They're serving *brownies* at the dance?

"No thanks." Brenda hurried away.

She moved through the shadows toward the deejay behind his table. "Play something good!" someone yelled. The deejay, a young man with slicked-back black hair and a black mustache, his head bobbing under large headphones, didn't seem to hear.

Where's Ted?

How could he disappear like that?

Weren't we *dancing* together?

She turned back to the dance floor. Is Ted dancing?

It was so hard to see.

"Hey, Brenda. Hi." A short girl with straight black hair down to her waist.

"Della? Hi. You see Ted?"

"I saw him dancing with you," Della said. "You lost him?"

"Yeah," Brenda replied, feeling dazed, out of sync. "Yeah. That's it, Della. I lost him."

"Try the Lost and Found!" Della joked, and laughed, a hearty laugh for such a tiny girl.

"Thanks."

She spotted Ted a short while later. Against the far wall near the double doors.

She didn't see Ted first. She saw the piled-up blonde hair, red in the shadowy lights.

She recognized the hair first. Halley's hair.

Then she saw Ted kissing Halley. The two

of them leaning against the tile wall. He had one arm around her bare shoulders.

What was that dress she was wearing, that short, clingy dress, down off the shoulders? Brenda had never seen it. Halley must have been saving it specially for the dance.

Specially for stealing Ted away.

Brenda moved closer, watching them kiss.

In front of everyone. In front of the whole school. Ted, her date, kissing Halley, her cousin.

No *wonder* everyone had been staring at Brenda all week!

I *am* in the wrong dream, she thought sadly.

And then, as she stood in the middle of the floor, uncertain of what to do next or where to go, everything became even more unreal, even more dreamlike.

And Noah appeared, as if out of nowhere.

He was wearing a shiny, loose-fitting sport shirt over neatly creased chinos. His dress-up outfit?

He moved quickly. Too quickly. As if he were floating toward the kissing couple, as if he were propelled.

From one dream into another.

It just didn't seem real to Brenda.

Noah had such a look of rage on his face.

There he was, as Brenda stared, pulling Ted away.

Ted pulled back. He shoved Noah. Noah shoved Ted.

Halley was talking quickly, her face twisted in surprise. She raised her hands to her face.

Was she screaming at Noah? Was she just screaming?

The music grew louder. It echoed on all sides. The shadows began to whir. Faster and faster. Inside the tornado.

And Noah was pulling the front of Ted's shirt. And Ted shoved Noah into the wall.

How did they get outside after that?

Brenda didn't remember following them out. But she suddenly realized she was cold, without her jacket. It was much darker now. The sky above was charcoal-gray. There were no stars. No shimmering lights bouncing off the silver balloons.

She had chased after them. Noah pulling Ted. Ted pushing Noah. Halley running in her shiny red pumps. The pumps that matched the sexy dress.

Everyone shouting at once.

"Stop it! Stop it now!" Halley's voice so shrill, so angry.

"Stop it!"

But now they were in the parking lot behind the school. Narrow beams of white light shooting onto the parked cars from tall poles.

And Noah shoved Ted hard into the wire fence. The fence rattled in protest and shook, holding Ted like a spiderweb.

But Ted pulled free and his fist shot out, hitting air.

Noah kicked at him. Ted sprang forward with a loud grunt, shoved Noah hard, and sent him sprawling backwards over the hood of a white Buick Skylark.

They groaned and uttered quiet sobs as they went at each other.

And across the parking lot, huddled between two cars, Brenda watched in mute horror. As if watching a dream.

Watched Halley pose under a white spotlight. Her hair so blonde, her dress so shiny, red as fresh blood.

Halley posed under the light and watched the fight.

Brenda trembled when she saw Halley's face. The pleased smile. The joy. The total joy on Halley's face.

Halley was enjoying the fight so much.

That's when Brenda turned away.

The smile on Halley's face made Brenda turn away, her stomach churning.

She could still hear the grunts and cries of the fight behind her. She raised her hands to cover her ears, and started to run.

Between the parked cars, then across the wide open aisle of the parking lot. Behind the school now. The gym door open just a crack, the music seeping out like air from the mouth of a balloon.

Leaving the pounding drums and guitars behind, Brenda ran into darkness.

She was running across someone's yard now, the tall grass wet with dew. She crossed a street and kept running, her heart pounding, the streetlights bobbing and tilting ahead of her.

Okay, she thought.

Okay okay okay okay okay okay.

I'm okay, she thought, her shoes pounding the sidewalk.

I'm okay okay okay.

No more dreams. No more illusions. No more living in a dreamworld for you, Brenda.

You're okay okay okay okay.

And you know what you have to do.

It didn't take long to run home. It didn't take long to push open the front door and run up to her room and grab the phone and punch in Traci's number.

Traci picked up on the second ring, startled

by Brenda's breathless greeting. "Brenda —
are you home already? Dina's here. What happened? Why are you home so early? Why do
you sound so weird?"

"You know our murder plot?" Brenda cried
into the phone, gasping to catch her breath.
"You know our plot to murder Halley? Let's
do it, okay? Let's *really* kill her!"

Chapter 14

"Are these cool or what?" Traci strutted around the room, waving the bouquet of peacock feathers.

"They're really beautiful," Dina said, reaching out to run her hand down one blue-and-green feather.

"But how are you going to sew them on your costume?" Brenda asked.

Traci stopped strutting and lowered the long feathers to her side. "Well . . . I thought maybe you'd help me, Bren. You're such a good seamstress. When it comes to sewing, I'm all thumbs."

It was a gray afternoon. The three girls had shared a lunch of tomato soup and peanut butter sandwiches. Then they'd made their way up to Brenda's room to talk.

Dina was wearing a black-and-white-striped sweater over faded jeans. Traci, her black hair pulled straight back in a ponytail, wore loose-fitting gray sweats. Brenda had on an enormous, old, white dress shirt of her father's over black tights.

"I think we have to wrap the stems together somehow, then sew them onto the back of the costume," Brenda said thoughtfully, staring hard at the feathers bobbing on their long stems. "Maybe if we cut the stems — "

She was interrupted by Randy, who barged into the room, a smear of peanut butter on his cheek. "Anyone want to play *Prince of Persia*? It's a great game!"

"What's *Prince of Persia*?" Traci asked.

"I just *told* you. It's a game," Randy replied impatiently. "You know. A computer game."

"We don't have time for games, Randy," Brenda said sharply. She put her hands on his shoulders and turned him around. "Take a walk, okay?"

"Hey!" He squirmed out of her grasp. "Maybe *they* want to play!"

"Not right now." Traci and Dina shook their heads.

"We're busy," Brenda told him. "Get lost. Really."

"You're a jerk," Randy told her.

"I know," Brenda replied. She gave him a push toward the door. He made an ugly face at her, then hurried out. As soon as he was gone, Brenda closed the door, making sure it clicked shut.

"Were we like that when we were ten?" she asked her friends.

"Girls are different," Dina replied.

"I think he's cute," Traci said, smiling.

Brenda sighed and dropped down onto the edge of her bed. "Maybe we should all go play *Prince of Persia* instead of talking about what we're going to talk about."

Traci's smile faded. "Were you serious? I mean, about what you said on the phone?"

"Deadly serious," Brenda replied, narrowing her eyes.

"Oh, wow." Traci dropped the peacock feathers on the dressertop and lowered herself onto the desk chair.

"We're going to plan a real murder?" Dina asked, lowering her voice. She stood by the window, leaning against the frame, her hands in her jeans pockets. She looked very pale in the gray light from outside.

"We've already planned it," Brenda told her.

"But that was just for fun," Dina insisted.

"Murdering Halley *will* be fun," Brenda said matter-of-factly.

Traci laughed, nervous laughter. "I can't be-lieve you can sit here so calmly and talk about killing your own cousin like it's *nothing*."

Brenda shifted her weight on the bed. She twisted the opal ring on her middle finger as she talked, her eyes on the window. "I've thought about it a lot. A *lot*, Traci. I know we can do it."

"Using our murder plot?" Dina asked, staring hard at Brenda as if trying to discover how serious she was.

"We can do it," Brenda repeated. "Sit down, Dina. You're making me nervous, standing like that."

Dina snickered. "Planning a murder *doesn't* make you nervous? But me standing here does?"

"Just sit down," Brenda replied sharply. "Come on. We've got a lot to talk about."

Traci and Dina both moved, and the three girls clustered together on top of the pink quilted bedspread. Traci had a peacock feather in her hand and kept pulling it through her fingers.

"Are you sure you can't just *talk* to Halley?" Dina asked, smoothing the bedspread with one hand. "I mean, if you tell her — "

"Tell her *what*?" Brenda snapped shrilly. "Tell her that I don't want maggoty meat in my bed anymore? Tell her that I'd really prefer it if she kept the headless, decaying birds to herself? Tell her that I don't need her stealing my boyfriends and deliberately wrecking my car?"

"Okay, okay," Traci said soothingly, patting Brenda's heaving shoulders. "Calm down, Bren. We know what you've been through." She sighed. "Halley stole my boyfriend, too."

"There's no *point* in talking to her!" Brenda screamed at Dina.

"I'm sorry," Dina said softly, casting a troubled glance at Traci. "I just thought — "

"Killing Halley will be so easy," Brenda interrupted, her green eyes lighting up excitedly. "I've got it all planned. We just switch costumes. At the party. No one will know who did it. And then — "

"Whoa!" Traci cried. "Back up, Bren. Not so fast. What do you mean, switch costumes?"

Brenda sighed impatiently. "Look. Everyone knows I'm going to be a clown, right? I've told everyone I know, everyone I invited to the party."

"Yeah. So?" Traci demanded.

"So everyone knows that you're going to be a peacock," Brenda continued, talking rapidly.

"If we can get my tail to stay on," Traci said, running the long feather through her fingers.

"And Dina's going to be a monk, right?" Brenda said. "So, what if we switch costumes?

Look." She jumped to her feet and hurried over to the dresser. Crouching down, she pulled open the bottom drawer. After a brief search, she pulled a small bundle out from under a pile of sweaters.

"What's that? Another costume?" Traci asked.

Brenda nodded, an excited smile on her face. She unwrapped the costume, and an ugly mask dropped onto the bed. "It's a Frankenstein costume," she told them. "I bought it at a party store yesterday." She held up the green rubber Frankenstein mask.

"Who's going to wear *that*?" Traci asked.

"I am," Brenda announced. She picked up the mask and started to roll up the costume around it. "Don't you see? I tell everyone I'm going to be a clown. But, instead, I wear the Frankenstein costume. Then *you* wear the clown costume. So everyone thinks you're me. And Dina can wear the peacock costume, so everyone will think she's you."

"So we're all in different costumes. Then what?" Traci demanded, a bewildered expression on her face. She tugged nervously at her black ponytail. Across from her, Dina remained silent, her eyes on Brenda.

"Then I kill Halley," Brenda said impatiently, as if it were obvious. "I stab her. In the chest. You know. In her gorilla suit. In that heavy costume, no one will even see the blood."

"Where will you get the knife?" Dina asked softly.

Brenda scowled. "That's no problem. My parents have these really sharp kitchen knives. I'll use one of those. Then, see, I'll change my costume before anyone even realizes that Halley has been stabbed."

"You'll change into what?" Traci asked.

"Into Dina's monk robe," Brenda replied. "See? I have it all figured out. No one will know who is what. I'll stab Halley as Frankenstein. And then the Frankenstein will completely disappear. And if anyone questions why the three of us are in each other's costumes, we'll say we did it at the last minute as a goof. Just for fun."

Brenda stared expectantly at her two friends, waiting for their reaction. "It's perfect, isn't it?" she asked excitedly.

"There's just one problem," Dina said in a whisper.

"Huh? Problem?" Brenda asked, frowning.

"Yeah," Dina replied, climbing to her feet. "I'm not doing it."

"Dina — " Brenda started.

"No. No way," Dina insisted, shaking her head. She started toward the bedroom door, then turned back to Brenda. Her face was pale, her lower lip trembling. "I can't, Brenda. I can't do it. I know you hate Halley. And I know she's done some horrible things to you. But I just can't do this."

"Dina, listen — " Brenda pleaded.

"No. No. No," Dina said with growing emotion. "I won't try to talk you out of it. And I won't tell anyone what you're planning, or what I know. But I won't do it, Brenda. I won't be part of it. I can't murder someone. . . . I just *can't!*"

Dina turned and hurried out of the room, closing the door hard behind her.

Brenda sat very still, listening to Dina's footsteps descend the stairs. When she heard the front door slam, she got up and walked to her closet. "Here. Try this on, Traci," she said, pulling out her red-and-white clown costume.

"Huh? Try it on? Now?" Traci climbed to her feet, a bewildered expression on her face.

"It isn't quite finished," Brenda said, holding it up for Traci to admire. "I still have to put the big buttons on the front. But we have to make sure it fits you."

"You mean — ?" Traci started.

"It'll actually be easier with just the two of us," Brenda said, giving her friend a reassuring smile. "We didn't really need Dina, but I thought she'd be hurt if we left her out."

"We're still going to switch costumes?" Traci demanded.

"Yeah. Right," Brenda replied, shoving the clown costume into Traci's arms. "You'll be the clown, and I'll be the peacock."

"But, Brenda, what if — ?"

Brenda had her head tilted, a thoughtful expression on her face. "Know what?" she said, ignoring Traci's reluctance. "I'll sew a new Frankenstein costume. I'll make it really big. You know. Big and baggy. So it'll fit over the peacock costume. Then, after I stab Halley, I can go into the other room and tear it off — and I'll be all set to reappear as the peacock."

"And you'll hide the Frankenstein costume?" Traci asked.

"Yeah. Sure." A smile spread across Brenda's face. "I'm going to shove it down the laundry chute. No one will ever think to look there."

Traci chewed her lower lip. "I don't know, Bren . . ."

Brenda gave Traci a gentle shove. "Don't just stand there. Try on the clown costume. We don't have time to waste."

Traci held the costume up in front of her. "I think it'll fit," she said in a quiet voice.

Brenda's grin widened. "I can't believe Halley is going to wear that big gorilla suit. She's

made it so much easier for me to kill her! It's
the first thing she ever did for me!" Brenda
snickered. "Do you believe it, Traci? After next
Saturday, Halley will be gone. Gone! And I can
breathe again!"

Brenda did an energetic twirl. Traci stared
reluctantly at the clown costume.

Below Brenda's room on the first floor of the
house, a figure stood in the narrow hallway
between the living room and the kitchen. She
stood very still, very straight, as if paralyzed.

The figure was Halley. She had been standing in the hallway for a long time, under the
air vent that led up to Brenda's room.

And she had heard every word that was said
in Brenda's room.

Chapter 15

That evening, Mr. and Mrs. Morgan went out for dinner with friends. Brenda had a pizza delivered. She and Randy sat across from each other at the dining room table. Halley sat at the end of the table, as far away from Brenda as she could get. She nibbled at her pizza slice, avoiding Brenda's stare.

"Can we play *Prince of Persia* after dinner?" Randy pleaded. "Please!"

"I can't," Brenda replied curtly. "I have to go to the mall to get some sewing supplies." She swallowed a pepperoni slice. "Want to come with me?"

Randy shook his head dispiritedly. "No way. I don't want to go to any sewing store." He pulled another slice from the box. "Will you play with me when you get back?"

"Maybe," Brenda replied, only half-hearing

her brother, her mind on other things.

Randy turned to Halley. "How about you? Can you play with me?"

"I'm not good at computer games," Halley said quietly. "Do you have checkers or chess or something?"

"Boring," Randy muttered, pulling the cheese off his slice. He always pulled the cheese off and ate it separately.

Brenda stared down the table at her cousin, an unfriendly sneer on her face. "What's going on, Halley? No date tonight?"

Halley lowered her eyes to her pizza and didn't reply.

"No boys fighting over you tonight?" Brenda teased, her tone cold and bitter.

Halley didn't reply. Her expression remained frozen in a tight frown. She picked up her plate, stood up, and carried it away from the table.

"Why were you so mean to her?" Randy demanded.

"*I'm* not mean. *She's* mean," Brenda replied curtly.

"You're always mean to her," Randy told his sister.

"You don't know what you're saying," Brenda said.

"She didn't do anything to you," Randy argued.

"Give me a break," Brenda moaned.

"Saturday night at the mall," Brenda muttered to herself, shaking her head. She had driven around the parking lot three times before she found a parking place. "Everyone I know is probably hanging out here tonight."

She glanced at the sign listing the movies playing at the tenplex. I should've made plans with Traci or Dina to go to a movie, she thought, climbing out of the car and slamming the door. She pulled her jacket collar up around her neck.

No. Who can concentrate on a movie?

She lowered her head against the gusting wind and, glancing up at the starless purple sky, her hands in her jeans pockets, began making her way quickly across the parking lot.

The sewing store was off in a corner near the auto service center. I can probably duck in and out without running into anyone I know, she told herself.

She wasn't in a social mood.

She wanted to get the threads and buttons she needed and hurry back to her room. To think.

She had a lot to think about.

A crash, followed by a metallic clatter and a loud shout, made Brenda utter a strangled cry and spin around.

Two rows behind her, a stationwagon had backed into a shopping cart.

Calm down, she scolded herself. *You nearly jumped out of your skin!*

Her heart was still pounding.

Guess I'm a little jumpy, she thought, taking a deep breath and holding it.

She pulled open the heavy glass door and stepped through a blast of warm air, into the brightly lit corridor.

WIN A NEW CORVETTE!

The banner caught her eye as she entered.

Beneath the banner, encased inside a box of clear plastic, was a shiny, red Corvette.

And standing to the side of the display case, admiring the car, were Ted and Noah.

"Huh?" Brenda stopped short. She wasn't sure she was seeing correctly. Her eyes still hadn't adjusted to the brightness of the mall courtyard.

"Whoa." It was definitely Ted and Noah.

She watched as Noah gave Ted a playful shove into the plastic display case. Ted said

something, and the two of them laughed
heartily.

"I don't believe this," Brenda muttered to
herself.

She pictured the two boys going at each
other in the dark parking lot the night before,
trying to kill each other, battling for the fair
Halley, as Halley preened in the spotlight, enjoying their ferocious battle.

And now here were Ted and Noah, the best
of pals, kidding around, joking and laughing
together.

Boys are weird, Brenda thought.

Boys are jerks, to put it in Randy's language.

Brenda stared at them, standing in the center of the wide aisle. She felt a wave of disgust
rise over her.

Ted is such a creep.

How could he do that to me? Leave me by
myself in the middle of the dance floor to go
make out with Halley. In front of everyone!

He hadn't even phoned her later.

The creep. The jerk.

She had a sudden urge to start another fight,
to slug Ted in the jaw, to hit him as hard as
she could. To hurt him the way he had hurt
her.

A picture flashed into her mind. Her fist had
landed squarely on Ted's jaw, and his teeth

were flying in the air. Like in a cartoon.

She couldn't help but laugh.

But then she remembered she didn't want Ted and Noah to see her. She turned abruptly and began jogging away from them, in the direction of the sewing store.

Too late.

"Hey — Brenda! Brenda!"

She kept jogging, pretending she didn't hear Ted's surprised cries. "Whoa!" Brenda nearly plowed into a woman pushing a baby stroller.

"Brenda — wait up!"

Ted was beside her now, breathing hard, pushing back his brown hair, his dark eyes locked on hers. "Brenda. Hi."

She stopped and scowled at him. She didn't say a word.

"I — I was going to call you, Bren," he stammered, fiddling with the cuffs of his sweatshirt.

"How did you enjoy the dance?" she asked with a bitter sneer.

"Uh . . . yeah." He lowered his eyes. "Listen, I'm sorry. I . . . messed up."

"Yeah, you did," she said coldly. "You messed up, Ted." She glanced over his shoulder. Noah had lingered at the Corvette display. He was pretending to still be interested in the car.

Ted swallowed hard. "I guess if I said I'm sorry — "

"It wouldn't do you any good."

He raised his eyes to hers. His cheeks turned bright pink. "But I really am sorry, Bren," he said.

"Yeah. Me, too," she replied coldly. "I'm real sorry."

He kicked at an already-flattened paper cup on the floor. "You know, you could give me another chance," he said softly. "It won't happen again. Really. I swear to you, Bren. It won't happen again."

"That's for sure!" she declared bitterly. She started to walk away, taking rapid strides.

"No, wait." He hurried to keep up with her. "Your Halloween party. I guess you don't want me to come now. I guess — "

Brenda had a sudden idea. It was so mean, so completely cruel, so *bad*, it made her laugh out loud.

Ted seemed to shrink back. He was blushing bright scarlet. "Well, I just . . . uh . . . wanted to say I'm sorry. Really."

"You can come to the party," Brenda told him, still snickering.

His dark eyes widened in shock. "Huh? I can?"

"Yeah. Sure," Brenda said. "Just about everyone from McKinley is coming. You might as well come, too, Ted. We'll all be in costumes, and it'll be such a mob, I won't even know you're there."

She could see the hurt flicker in his eyes.

"How about if I stay and help you clean up afterwards or something?" he suggested.

She frowned. "I don't think so. Do you have a costume?"

"Not yet," he said, glancing back at Noah, who was still pretending to study the Corvette.

"Well, you can do me one favor," Brenda told him.

"Sure. Anything," he said eagerly.

"Come as Frankenstein."

"Huh?"

"There are some good Frankenstein costumes at the party store over there." Brenda pointed. "Come as Frankenstein, okay? I made a bet with Randy."

Ted scratched his head. "A bet?"

"Yeah. I bet him there would be a Frankenstein at the party," Brenda said, surprising herself at what a good liar she was becoming. "Randy thinks that only Freddy Kreugers will show up. No Frankensteins. So, go get one of those Frankenstein costumes, okay?"

A smile spread over Ted's handsome face. "Okay, Bren. You got it."

She grinned back at him, so pleased with herself, she felt she might burst.

"Hey, Ted!" Noah called from the car display. "What's happening?"

"I've got to get going," Ted said, gesturing for Noah to hold on a minute. "Listen, Bren — "

"I know. You're real sorry about last night," Brenda said sarcastically.

"Yeah. I am. Really," he said, avoiding her hard stare.

"See you at the party, Frankenstein. And tell Noah he's too short for a Corvette," Brenda joked. "He'd have to sit in a booster seat to see over the steering wheel."

Ted chuckled. "That's cold!" he declared. "That's really cold. See you." He gave her a quick wave, and loped off toward Noah.

You don't know cold, Brenda thought, smiling.

Running into Ted hadn't been such a bad thing after all. She couldn't wait to tell Traci and Dina how she had maneuvered Ted into a Frankenstein costume, the same kind of costume the killer would be wearing.

What a riot!

Thinking about it cheered Brenda up a lot.

At the sewing store, empty on a Saturday night except for Brenda and a bored salesgirl, she found the buttons she needed to complete her clown costume, and picked up some thick foam padding and several spools of thread.

She looked forward to spending the rest of the evening sewing. Sewing always relaxed her. And it gave her time to think. She always did her best thinking with a needle in her hand.

As Brenda drove home, she thought about the afternoon. It had gone really well, she thought.

Dina's decision not to join in had come as a surprise. But then Dina had always defended Halley since the day Halley arrived. Dina had some kind of soft spot for Halley, Brenda decided.

Was it because Dina's parents had gone through a terrible divorce and a long, drawn-out custody battle, just like Halley's parents were doing now?

Brenda shuddered, thinking about Dina. They had been such close, close friends. But during the divorce, Brenda just couldn't bear to be with Dina or to see her. It was just too sad.

Too horribly sad.

Brenda had been glad when the mess was all settled, and Dina was happily living with her mother, and she and Traci and Dina could all be friends again.

Yes, she had been very glad.

But now Dina was breaking away from the trio again, refusing to join in.

Too bad, Brenda thought unhappily. Too bad . . .

But I guess I can understand.

She pulled her father's Pontiac up the driveway and cut the engine and the lights. Then, grabbing up her package, she hurried into the house, eager to start sewing.

To Brenda's surprise, the light was on in her bedroom.

She hesitated at the doorway and peered in.

Someone was sitting on her bed. Halley!

Under the harsh yellow light from the ceiling lamp, Halley turned and glared at Brenda, her blue eyes brimming with hatred. "Come in, Brenda," she said in a tight, hard voice. "I've been waiting for you."

Chapter 16

Brenda hesitated, one hand on the doorframe, the other gripping her bag from the sewing store. She stared at Halley, studying her face.

Halley's hair, which usually fell freely around her head, was tied tightly back. Her eyes were narrowed as they gazed at Brenda. Her lips were pursed, her expression set as if chiseled in cold stone.

"Uh . . . I thought you were playing with Randy," Brenda said suspiciously, still not entering her own room.

"We played some games, but Randy got bored. Now he's watching TV downstairs," Halley replied, her expression not softening.

"Well, what are you doing in here, Halley?" Brenda demanded. Her voice trembled. She cleared her throat. "What are you doing in my room?"

Halley stared at her coldly and didn't reply. Her eyes burned into Brenda's.

Brenda tried to read her thoughts, but couldn't.

What is going on here? she wondered. *What does Halley want?*

"I . . . uh . . . have to do some sewing now," Brenda said, holding up the brown paper bag.

"Come in," Halley replied, her eyes locked on Brenda's, forcing Brenda to look away. "We have to talk."

Taking a deep breath, Brenda stepped into the room and tossed her package onto the desk. Staring suspiciously at Halley, she crossed her arms over her chest.

"What do we have to talk about?" Brenda demanded with a sneer.

Halley stood up suddenly, so suddenly, that Brenda uttered a short cry of surprise. Halley moved toward Brenda, her features set in a menacing frown.

What is she going to do? Brenda wondered, feeling a tremor of fear start in the pit of her stomach and radiate through her body.

Why is she staring at me like that?

Why is she coming toward me with that threatening look on her face?

Swallowing hard, Brenda was about to turn

and run from the room when she saw the tears glisten in the corners of Halley's eyes.

Halley stopped.

The tears swelled, then dropped onto Halley's pale cheeks.

Halley opened her mouth to speak, but no sound came out.

To Brenda's shock, Halley's hard expression crumbled. The tears ran down Halley's cheeks and she began to sob, her slender shoulders heaving up and down.

"Halley — " Brenda started.

"Have I really been so hateful?" Halley blubbered through her sobs.

"Huh? Halley, I — " Brenda's voice trailed off. She was too shocked to speak.

Halley's hard expression — it was just an attempt to hold back the tears.

But now the tears were flowing, and Halley couldn't keep them back. "Have I really been so hateful?" she repeated. "So hateful that you want to *kill* me?"

She *heard!* Brenda realized, feeling a cold stab of dread in her chest. "Halley, listen to me" — she backed up and quietly closed the bedroom door — "Listen — "

"I didn't mean to be so horrible!" Halley wailed. "I — I thought you and I — I mean, I thought we could be friends. I thought — " She dropped onto the bed and covered her face with her hands, her shoulders trembling.

She heard. She heard. She heard everything! Brenda realized. Feeling dizzy, she lowered herself to the other side of the bed and waited for Halley to stop crying.

After a while, Halley's sobs quieted. She wiped the tears off her cheeks with her hands. Brenda walked over to the dresser and carried the tissue box to her cousin. She sat down again as Halley dabbed at her eyes with a tissue, breathing hard, avoiding Brenda's stare.

Finally, she raised her eyes to Brenda. "I really didn't want this to happen," she said, speaking slowly, pronouncing each word carefully, forcing back the urge to start sobbing again.

Brenda didn't reply. She didn't know what to say. She waited for her cousin to continue.

"I really thought you and I would be friends," Halley said, clutching a wadded-up tissue in her hand. "Best buddies. I didn't mean to be so awful. I didn't mean for any of it to happen."

"But it did," Brenda said flatly.

Halley nodded. "I was just so scared, Brenda. So insecure. I — I was so freaked about having to live away from home," she stammered. "Away from my friends. And my — and my parents."

"Yes. I see," Brenda said uncomfortably.

"I was so worried about my parents," Halley continued. "My mom especially. She blamed herself. I knew she did. And she was so dependent on Daddy. And on me. And now . . . I didn't know how she'd get along. I mean, I didn't know if she *could* get along. I was just so scared, you see."

Halley raised the tissue to her nose and wiped it. Some strands of blonde hair had come free from the ribbon that held them. Halley's eyes were red-rimmed and watery, and her cheeks were tear-stained.

"And when I came here to stay," Halley continued, turning her gaze to the darkness outside the window, "I was in really bad shape. I mean, my head was just messed up. And you weren't friendly, Brenda. You weren't. You didn't want me here, I could tell."

"Now, wait — " Brenda protested weakly.

"No. It's true," Halley insisted. "I was an intruder. You made me feel like an intruder. Maybe I imagined some of it. Maybe I exaggerated. But I don't think so. There I was, staying in your room, meeting your friends —

and you didn't want me. I could feel you didn't want me, Brenda."

"Halley — I'm sorry," Brenda said sincerely. She reached out to grab Halley's arm, but Halley pulled away.

"No. I'm sorry," Halley replied. "I'm the one who's sorry. I'm the one who took away your boyfriend, who tried to show you, to teach you a lesson for rejecting me."

"You took away Traci's boyfriend, too," Brenda accused.

Halley's tear-stained cheeks reddened. "I really can't explain it," she told Brenda. "I can't defend it. I don't know why I did it. I guess I wanted to prove that I was as good as you and your friends, that I could fit in, too. I guess I wanted to show you that I didn't care if you accepted me, if you wanted me here or not. I could do whatever I wanted."

Halley uttered a long sigh. "I was just so mixed up. So hurt and so bitter. I wasn't being myself. I *couldn't* be myself. I had to be on guard all the time. I was so scared, Brenda, so scared. . . ." Her voice trailed off.

The two girls stared at each other in silence.

Finally, Halley said, "Please forgive me. Okay?"

She slid forward and wrapped her arms

around Brenda's shoulders in a tight, emotional hug. "Forgive me. Let's start all over. Okay, Brenda? Okay?"

"Okay," Brenda whispered, and hugged Halley back.

As she hugged her cousin, Brenda was startled to find that she had tears in her own eyes.

Halley is really sincere, Brenda realized.

She really wants for us to be close.

She really is sorry for everything that has happened.

What a shame, Brenda thought.

What a shame that I have to go ahead with my plan anyway.

Chapter 17

"Is she really going to do it?" Dina asked.

Traci, standing in her kitchen, her back against the yellow wallpaper, twisted the phone cord around her wrist. "I don't know," she replied quietly. "What do you think?"

On the other end of the line, Dina remained silent. Traci could hear only a loud crackling sound.

"What's that noise?" Traci asked, freeing her hand from the cord, then tangling it around her wrist again.

"Oh. Sorry," Dina said. "I'm chewing gum."

"So loud?" Traci demanded.

"I guess I'm nervous or something," Dina admitted. "Hold on." She removed the wad of blue bubble gum from her mouth and set it down on her desk beside the phone.

"I think Brenda is very serious," Traci said, tracing the name Brenda on the kitchen wall with her finger. "I think she's going ahead with the plan."

"When did you talk to her about it?" Dina demanded anxiously.

"Well . . . I talked to her yesterday at lunch. But we didn't talk about Halley," Traci replied.

"She didn't mention Halley?" Dina asked.

"No. Not once."

"So maybe Brenda's decided not to go ahead with it," Dina said. She picked up the blue wad of gum and nervously stuck it and unstuck it to the desktop.

"No. I really think all systems are go," Traci said dryly.

Dina uttered a soft moan. "I'm just so scared for her, Traci. Shouldn't we do something?"

"Like what?" Traci demanded, fingering the name Halley on the yellow wallpaper.

"Like call the police?" Dina asked, her shrill voice revealing her fear.

"They wouldn't believe it," Traci said coolly. "And Brenda would just deny it."

"Well, maybe we should warn Halley," Dina suggested. "Or tell Brenda's parents what Brenda is planning to do."

"They wouldn't believe it, either," Traci said. "They would never believe that Brenda was planning to murder Halley."

"But if we tell them the whole thing — "

"If we tell them the whole thing," Traci interrupted, "Brenda will say the murder plot is just a school assignment. She'll show them the paper we wrote up. And that will be that."

There was a long silence at Dina's end. "I'm just so scared," she said finally.

Traci snickered. "I feel bad for Ted. That's such a mean trick Brenda is playing on him. Having him come to the party in a Frankenstein costume."

"I know," Dina replied. "If anyone sees the Frankenstein stab the gorilla, they'll think Ted did it."

"Brenda really has a *cold* sense of humor," Traci said, tracing the word *cold* on the wall with her finger.

"I keep thinking maybe I'll stay home," Dina said. "I mean, just skip the party."

"But you're not involved," Traci told her.

"I don't want to witness a murder!" Dina exclaimed. "Are you and Brenda still trading costumes?"

"Yeah," Traci told her. "I'm going to be the clown. She's going to be the peacock."

Dina groaned. "She's going to do it. I know it!"

Traci remained silent.

"What are you thinking?" Dina demanded. "Come on. Spill. What are you thinking, Traci?"

"I was thinking about Noah," Traci admitted after a long pause. And then she added bitterly, "The little rat."

She heard a sharp intake of breath on Dina's end of the line. "You *want* Brenda to kill Halley, *don't* you?" Dina accused. "You really *want* her to go ahead with it?"

"Yeah. Maybe I do," Traci confessed.

"What a mess!" Brenda declared.

"Well, we're done," Halley said. "That's the last one."

Brenda raised her hands in the air. They were covered with shreds of orange pumpkin. Glancing down, she saw that the sleeve of her sweater was stained orange.

"Look at that gunk," Halley exclaimed, pointing to the pile of pumpkin flesh and seeds on the newspaper, which they had spread over the kitchen table.

Brenda laughed. "You have seeds in your hair."

Halley pointed at Brenda. "You have pumpkin stuff on your forehead."

They both laughed.

"Whose idea was this, anyway?" Brenda

asked, rolling her eyes. "I mean, *six* jack-o'-lanterns! I have to be crazy!"

"Well, we did it," Halley proclaimed happily. "Whew! I'm totally wrecked."

Both girls raised their eyes to the six grinning jack-o'-lanterns lined up across from them on the table.

"What an ugly mob scene," Brenda said, shaking her head.

"They'll look so pretty when they're lit up," Halley remarked. "Where are you going to put them?"

"On the floor. Against the living room wall," Brenda told her. "And I'm going to turn off all the lamps. So the only light in the room will come from the jack-o'-lanterns."

"It'll be neat," Halley said, straightening the top on one of the pumpkins.

"That one is totally lopsided," Brenda said, frowning.

"It gives it character," Halley said. "I think he's the scariest of the bunch."

"What makes you think it's a *he*?" Brenda demanded.

They both laughed again.

We've been getting along so well, Brenda thought. Halley has been such a big help this afternoon.

"Want to roast some pumpkin seeds?" Halley

asked, running her hand over the big pile of seeds.

"No way!" Brenda protested, making a face. "I never want to see a pumpkin or a pumpkin seed again. Really!"

By the time they cleaned up and carried the six pumpkins into the living room, they were even more covered with orange shreds. "First shower!" Brenda cried.

Halley pulled a wet pumpkin seed from her hair. "Okay, but hurry," she told her cousin. "This stuff is starting to smell. Yuck!"

Brenda hurried upstairs, her mind whirring with thoughts of the party. I'll put the hot cider on the table by the front door, she told herself. That way, kids can help themselves to cider as soon as they walk in.

Then they'll walk into the dark living room, lit only by the candlelight from the six jack-o'-lanterns. That's going to be so neat, Brenda thought, a pleased smile forming on her face.

She and Halley had strung long ribbons of black-and-orange crepe, crisscrossing them over the room to form a low ceiling.

It'll look spooky in the dark, Brenda told herself.

Black crepe.

She pictured the long spools of black crepe. *Like at a funeral*, she thought.

With all of the preparations, Brenda had almost forgotten about her plan.

Her smile fading, she entered her room to get undressed for her shower. The clown costume was suspended on a hanger over the closet door.

After my shower, I'll take it over to Traci's and make the switch with her, she thought grimly.

She turned away from the closet door — and gasped.

"Randy!" she shrieked.

Her brother lay sprawled facedown on the bed, his arms and legs outstretched, a dark puddle of blood beside him on the bedspread.

Chapter 18

"Randy?"

Brenda's throat tightened, cutting off her breath. Her knees buckled, and she grabbed the top of her desk to keep from falling.

This isn't happening, she thought.

My little brother isn't lying on my bed in a pool of blood.

She blinked several times, trying to clear away the image.

"Randy?" Her voice was a choked whisper.

Gasping for air, she stumbled toward her bed. And as she began to lean over her brother, her hands reaching for his shoulders, he raised his head from the pink bedspread and grinned at her.

"Gotcha!" he said softly.

"No!" Brenda cried, relief mixed with astonishment.

Randy uttered a high-pitched, gleeful giggle and began flopping around on her bed like a crazed fish.

"How *could* you?" Brenda shrieked, reaching for him and missing. "You scared me to death!"

Her cries of protest made Randy laugh even more joyfully. He flung himself down, bounced up, flung himself down again, using her bed for a trampoline.

As he jumped, reaching his hands up to touch the ceiling, the puddle of blood bounced off the bed and landed on the white shag rug.

Brenda picked it up and examined it. "Plastic blood?" she cried, waving it accusingly at her bouncing brother. "I don't believe I fell for plastic blood."

"I got it at the party store," Randy told her. "It looks real, doesn't it?" He grinned at her, a triumphant grin.

"Get out of here!" Brenda cried impatiently. "Off my bed! Come on — out!"

It took her several minutes to get him to stop bouncing. Finally, he ran out of the room, yelling, "Gotcha! Gotcha! Gotcha!" all the way down the stairs.

Brenda shook her head, letting her breath out slowly.

What a scare!

And just think, she told herself wistfully, tomorrow will be even scarier.

The guests began arriving a little after eight o'clock the next night. By nine o'clock, the shadowy living room was bursting with masked kids in an astounding array of costumes.

Brenda counted two Freddy Kreugers, complete with long, knifelike metal fingers; two mummies, who both started to come unraveled soon after arriving; and two kids wearing dark suits and masks of the President of the United States.

One girl, a senior named Alissa, didn't appear to be in costume. She was wearing a very short, silky blue party dress, but no mask. "Who are you supposed to be?" Brenda asked her, having to shout from behind her mask.

"I'm Cindy Crawford," Alissa replied, pointing to the mole she had painted above her upper lip.

Brenda laughed. "Nice costume."

The party was going well. The sweet aroma of the hot mulled cider floated over the room. The row of jack-o'-lanterns against the wall glowed eerily, casting strange shadows along the floor, sending flickering light up to the crepe paper ceiling just above everyone's heads.

Music pounded from the stereo. The gorilla circulated through the room, carrying a tray of tiny hot dogs in rolls. The monk stood hunched beside the fireplace, masked beneath her heavy, dark hood, leaning close to hear what a masked Princess Di was saying to her.

People kept running their hands over the tailfeathers of the peacock, much to the peacock's consternation. Finding it hard to move around in the crowded living room, the peacock eventually removed the tail, tossing it into the downstairs bedroom where all the coats had been draped over the bed.

Half an hour later, the crowded room had become hot and steamy. The candles in the jack-o'-lanterns had lowered. The grinning pumpkin heads sent out dim, flickering light over the dancing couples.

Having served the last of the cocktail hot dogs, the gorilla sat in a folding chair against the wall. The clown danced energetically across the room with one of the mummies. One of the Frankensteins had his arm around the bare shoulders of Cindy Crawford.

No one paid any attention as another Frankenstein stepped up beside the gorilla's chair.

No one saw the gleam of the kitchen knife in the Frankenstein's hand as it caught a flicker of candle light from the grinning jack-o'-lanterns.

Frankenstein's hand moved quickly. A swift, sideways move. And the knifeblade plunged into the gorilla's chest.

No one could hear the gorilla's strangled cry from beneath the heavy mask. Its arms shot straight out. It tried to rise.

Then it dropped heavily back onto the chair as the knife was pulled out.

In the flickering, orange light, no one saw the gorilla's head slump forward on its chest.

And no one paid any attention as the Frankenstein monster slipped quietly away, into the deep shadows.

Chapter 19

"Hey — look out!"

Someone screamed as one of the Presidents stumbled backwards, accidentally kicking over a jack-o'-lantern. "You'll set the rug on fire!"

The jack-o'-lantern grinned its jagged grin, sideways now, its orange light flickering dimly. A long-nosed witch bent to roll the pumpkin rightside up.

Someone changed the music to a frantic rap song. One of the black crepe streamers pulled loose from its tape and floated down over the dancers in the middle of the room.

Kids began pulling at it, stretching it until it tore. And then pulling down all the crepe streamers became the game of the moment. In seconds, the room was cluttered with torn scraps of black and orange.

And everyone was laughing.

Until a scream cut through the laughter.

At first, it sounded like part of the music. The scream repeated itself, rising over the angry, rhythmic rapping.

And then someone cut the stereo off. And the screams continued.

And everyone searched the shadowy room for the source of the screams. And saw the long-nosed witch tear off her rubber mask and point to the gorilla, slumped at such an odd angle in the folding chair.

"There's *blood*!" the witch cried, pointing to a dark puddle beneath the gorilla's chair.

Another scream. Cries of confusion. Hushed whispers.

The entire room seemed to freeze in horror. Only the shadows moved as the candles flickered at the floor.

The hushed whispers faded into silence.

The witch stared down at the puddle of blood, and all eyes followed her horrified gaze.

Someone laughed. A high-pitched laugh, a forced laugh. "It's a joke!" one of the mummies cried.

Someone else laughed. Voices rose in the heavy air.

"Sit up!" someone called to the gorilla.

"What a goof!"

"Yeah. It's a joke."

"I knew it. I wasn't scared."

"Who is it? Take off your mask!"

"You can get up now! You scared us already!"

"Who is it? Is it Brenda's cousin?"

"Yeah. It's Halley. Get up, Halley!"

But the gorilla didn't move.

And suddenly a figure was moving quickly through the room. The white-faced clown made its way up to the chair, arms outstretched.

"Halley?" the clown cried, and began to shake the gorilla by the shoulders. "Halley? Halley?"

No reply.

Letting go of the hairy shoulders, the clown wrapped both hands around the top of the gorilla mask, and tugged.

The mask pulled up easily.

The room echoed with screams as the face underneath was revealed. Eyes closed. Mouth gaping open. Copper-colored hair falling behind the lifeless head.

"It's Brenda!" the clown shrieked. "Oh, no! It's Brenda! And she's dead!"

Chapter 20

"Nooooooo!" A shrill scream cut through the shocked silence.

"Not Brenda! No! Not Brenda!"

As the clown grasped the gorilla mask, Brenda's head fell against the chairback with a hard *thonk*.

"She — she's been stabbed!" the clown managed to choke out. The gorilla mask fell from her hands and bounced on the carpet beside the puddle of blood.

Screams and cries.

The clown tore off her mask, revealing that she was Traci. Her eyes were wide with horror. She gasped for breath. "Not Brenda! It can't be Brenda!" she cried.

"Traci — you're wearing Brenda's costume!" someone yelled.

"Yes. I — uh — " Traci tried to reply. But her throat tightened, choking off her words.

"Somebody call the police!"

"Call 911!"

Frightened voices competed with sobs of horror.

"Brenda! Brenda!" Traci shook the lifeless figure again by the shoulders. Brenda's head bounced against the chairback.

Suddenly, the dark-robed monk burst through the tight crowd. Dina tossed back her hood. Her eyes were narrowed with fury. Raising her robed arm, she pointed an accusing finger at Traci.

"You killed her, Traci!" Dina declared. "You and your stupid murder plot! You killed Brenda!"

Chapter 21

The cries faded. The voices grew silent, as if the horror in the room had swallowed up all sound.

Brenda sat slumped in the stiff-backed chair, her pale face rising above the dark fur of the costume.

Traci and Dina faced each other from opposing sides of the lifeless body.

"You killed her, Traci!" Dina repeated.

Traci shrank back, hands to her face, eyes wide in disbelief. The light flickered across the white front of the clown suit Brenda had so carefully sewn.

"No!" Traci replied to Dina in a trembling voice. "I didn't kill anyone!"

A third figure moved to the front of the room. The peacock darted forward, removing the blue-and-green mask to reveal a bewildered-looking Halley.

"She forced me!" Halley cried, her eyes on Brenda. "Brenda forced me to switch costumes with her! I — I didn't understand why."

"Whoa!" Traci interrupted, staring suspiciously at Halley. "Brenda traded costumes with me. She took my peacock costume, and I took the clown costume."

"And then she gave *me* the peacock costume," Halley wailed. "She made me trade. Brenda took the gorilla suit!"

"But why — ?" Traci cried.

"Traci, you *idiot!*" Dina shrieked in fury. "You thought you were killing Halley — and you stabbed your best friend instead!"

"Noooo!" Traci uttered a shrill cry. She leapt to attack Dina. But Dina fell back against the fireplace.

"Stop! Stop it! Stop!" Halley shrieked.

And suddenly Traci was staring at Halley, her eyes narrowed in suspicion. "It was *you*, wasn't it!"

"Huh?" Halley's eyes widened in surprise.

"You *forced* Brenda to switch costumes with you, didn't you, Halley!"

"No way!" Halley screamed, her hands forming tight fists at her side. "No way, Traci! That's not the way it happened!"

"Yes!" Traci insisted, advancing on Halley.

"You made Brenda take the gorilla suit, Halley. And then *you* stabbed her!"

"Did someone call 911?" a girl cried.

"Where are Brenda's parents? Did someone call her parents?"

Traci and Halley stared at each other, their features set in accusation.

"I didn't stab anyone!" Halley declared through clenched teeth. "You plotted to kill *me*, Traci! I heard you! I heard every word. But your plot backfired. You killed the wrong girl!"

"Oh, no!" Traci protested. "No! No! No!" She took a menacing step toward Halley. "It wasn't me. How could I change into a Frankenstein costume so quickly? I couldn't!"

"Frankenstein costume!" someone shouted.

"Frankenstein?"

"Yes!" Traci declared. "Brenda was stabbed by someone in a Frankenstein costume." She lowered her voice sadly. "It was part of our plot."

"Then it was *Ted*!" Dina declared. "Ted stabbed Brenda!"

Cries of surprise rang through the room.

"There are two Frankensteins here," Traci said. "One of them is Ted. Where are you, Ted? Ted?"

Two Frankensteins stepped forward reluctantly.

They lifted their masks. Traci recognized Brad Mitchell and Tony Alexander.

"Ted? Where are you, Ted?" Traci cried.

"He's gone!" Dina exclaimed. "I *knew* he was the killer!"

Chapter 22

"Has anyone seen Ted?" Halley cried.

Hushed voices. Whispers. Someone was crying in the back of the room.

A mummy stepped forward, tugging away the gauze around his face. "Ted isn't here," he said.

"Noah! *You're* here?" Traci cried.

"Ted is home. He has the flu," Noah reported. "He's home sick. You can call his house. His parents will tell you."

"But that's impossible!" Traci declared. "He was supposed to be here. In the Frankenstein costume, and — "

"He couldn't come," Noah said, staring at Brenda sprawled in the chair. "He has the flu. It's true, Traci! I — I — "

Noah's face froze in horror.

He tried to cry out, but no sound would come from his throat.

Slowly, he raised his trembling hand to point toward the chair.

All eyes followed his terrified gaze.

The room echoed with screams and startled cries.

In the straight-backed chair, Brenda moved.

At first, it appeared to be the flickering of shadows from the bending candlelight.

But no.

The corpse was moving.

Brenda slowly raised her head above the dark gorilla body. She blinked and closed her mouth.

Slowly, slowly, Brenda sat up. And stared into the startled faces of her friends.

"Happy Halloween," Brenda told them in a lifeless, dry voice, so bitter, so angry.

Chapter 23

"The joke is over, and so is the party," Brenda announced, climbing to her feet. She picked up the plastic puddle of blood from the floor and raised it high to show everyone it wasn't real.

The room filled with startled screams and cries.

"She's alive!"

"It was just a joke?"

"How *could* she?"

"I don't believe it!"

"Brenda — are you okay?"

"What's the big idea? She wasn't stabbed?"

Ignoring the outcry, Brenda grabbed Halley's shoulder and pulled her close. "Halley — get everyone out of here, okay? Tell them all to go home."

Halley nodded solemnly and turned to obey Brenda's instructions.

Muttering in surprise and confusion, the guests began gathering their coats and preparing to leave.

As Halley ushered them out, Brenda made her way into the kitchen, waddling heavily in the furry gorilla suit, followed by Traci and Dina. In the harsh kitchen light, their faces were red and perspiring.

All three of them were breathing hard. All three started talking at once.

"You're alive! Brenda, you're alive!" Dina declared, her brown hair matted with sweat against her forehead.

"The plot is over," Brenda said coldly, training her eyes first on Dina, then looking at Traci. "I know which one of you tried to kill me."

"But, Brenda — !" Traci protested, her eyes wide with shock.

Without warning, Brenda lunged forward. She grabbed the front of Dina's monk robe and ripped it open.

"I knew it!" Brenda cried, her eyes on the green costume underneath.

Dina pulled angrily from Brenda's grasp. All three girls cried out as a rubber mask fell out from the sleeve of Dina's robe. It bounced to the linoleum and stared up at them. A green-and-black Frankenstein mask.

"I *stabbed* you!" Dina cried, turning her furious glance on Brenda. "I *stabbed* you, Brenda! Why aren't you dead?"

A bitter smile crossed Brenda's lips. "I knew it was you, Dina," she uttered in a low whisper.

"Why aren't you dead?" Dina wailed. "Why?"

"I'm a good seamstress, remember?" Brenda replied, her eyes burning angrily into Dina's. She patted the front of her costume. "I sewed a double-thick pad of foam rubber into this gorilla suit."

Dina groaned in anger. She glared at Brenda. "How did you know? How did you know it was me?"

"All those horrible things you did to me, Dina," Brenda replied, her voice revealing more sadness than anger. "All those horrible things . . ."

"You were supposed to think it was Halley," Dina cried bitterly.

Brenda shook her head. "At first I *did* think it was Halley," Brenda admitted. "But then I realized, Dina. I realized it was you."

"How?" Dina demanded, backing toward the kitchen door. "How did you know?"

"The blood on the wall," Brenda said, her eyes narrowed on Dina. "It had to be animal blood. The headless bird in the pumpkin. Another animal. The chunks of rotten meat in my bed. They were dog food, spoiled dog food." She swallowed hard. "I put it together, Dina. Your job. After school every day at the veterinarian's office. It was easy for you to get that stuff."

"You — you *knew?*" Dina cried, unable to conceal her shock. "You knew before the party?"

Suddenly, Halley burst into the room, her hair wild about her head, her face scarlet. "Everyone's gone," she announced. Then she turned on Dina. "What did I ever do to you?"

Dina ignored her, glaring coldly at Brenda.

"You thought *I* was in the gorilla suit," Halley cried. "You thought you were stabbing *me*, Dina. Why? I just don't get it!"

Dina remained silent. Finally, she turned to Halley. "I knew you weren't in the gorilla suit. I listened at the air vent. I heard you and Brenda trade costumes. I *knew* I was stabbing Brenda. Brenda deserves to die."

"Why, Dina?" Traci demanded, gripping the kitchen counter. "Brenda is your friend. She — "

"No!" Dina exploded. "She wasn't my friend when I needed her!"

"Huh?" Traci and Brenda both reacted with shock.

"When my parents were getting divorced, when they were fighting in court over me — where were you *then*, Brenda?" she demanded, spitting the words with rage. "Where were you then? You *abandoned* me! You disappeared. You dropped me, didn't you, when I needed you the most!"

"But, Dina, I — I — " Brenda was too shocked to think clearly.

"And then I saw you doing the same thing to Halley," Dina accused, her features twisted in rage. "I saw you shutting her out when she needed you, when she was in the same kind of trouble I'd been in. And it brought it all back, Brenda. It brought it all back, and I knew I had to make you pay."

Brenda felt a wave of guilt sweep away her anger. "Dina, I didn't realize — " she started.

"Save the apologies!" Dina snarled. "I wanted to frighten you, Brenda. I wanted to show you what it was like to be so frightened you can't stand it, so frightened you can't think straight!"

Dina's chest heaved. She gasped for air. "I wasn't going to kill you. I just wanted to scare you. But killing was *your* idea! When you and Traci decided to *really* kill Halley, you gave me the idea. You put the idea in my head. That's when I knew I had to kill you, Brenda!"

"But, Dina — " Brenda replied, taking a step toward her. "Traci and I *never* planned to murder Halley. That was just a trick, a trick to draw you out. That whole plot to murder Halley — it wasn't real. It was all for your benefit. We never planned to stab Halley. We just wanted to trick you into confessing."

"But we never thought you'd — you'd really stab Brenda!" Traci stammered.

"I still want to kill you!" Dina raged. "I do! I really do!" She uttered a snarl of rage and shoved Brenda hard against the kitchen counter. Then she took off, running into the living room, her heavy monk robe flowing behind her.

Brenda, Traci, and Halley darted after her. "Dina — stop!" Brenda called.

Into the shadowy living room.

Dina was nearly across the room when she stumbled over one of the flickering jack-o'-lanterns. She uttered an angry cry as she toppled forward onto the floor.

"Dina — wait!"

Tangled in the long robe, Dina struggled to climb to her feet. "Let me *go*!" she shrieked.

She reached down, tried to untangle the robe. And stared into the tilted jack-o'-lantern. It grinned up at her, a jagged, laughing, evil grin.

Staring into its glowing eyes, Dina began to scream. Shrieking and sobbing, she struggled toward the front door, crawling on her hands and knees.

And then two dark-uniformed policemen were in the doorway, blocking Dina's path. "What's going on here? Who called 911?"

"I feel so bad," Brenda said later, her hands around a white mug of steaming hot chocolate. "I had no idea Dina had such resentment. Such *hatred*. I didn't deliberately drop Dina as a friend when her parents were divorcing. It was all such a mess back then. I really thought she wanted to be alone."

Halley shook her head sadly. She was seated across from Brenda at the kitchen table. She took a sip of her hot chocolate. "Ow. It's hot."

The house was silent. Everyone else had gone. Brenda's parents were picking up Randy at his friend's house and would soon be home.

"The police were very gentle and understanding with Dina," Halley said quietly, staring into her cup.

"She'll get the help she needs," Brenda said. She raised her mug and held it up toward her cousin. "Happy Halloween," she said wearily.

Halley raised her mug and clicked it against Brenda's. "It *is* a happy Halloween in a way," she said thoughtfully. "At least, things are different now. I mean, between you and me."

"Yeah. I guess you could say that you and I have finally taken off our masks," Brenda replied.

Halley sighed and gazed toward the cluttered living room. "Let's clean up tomorrow," she said.

Brenda laughed. "I think we're starting to understand each other really well!"

About the Author

R.L. STINE is the author of more than three dozen mysteries for young people, all of which have been best-sellers. Recent Scholastic horror titles include *The Baby-sitter III*, *The Dead Girlfriend*, and *The Hitchhiker*.

In addition, he is the author of two popular monthly series: *Goosebumps* and *Fear Street*.

Bob lives in New York City with his wife, Jane, and thirteen-year-old son, Matt.

THRILLERS